DATE DUE

JUL 1 1 1996	
MAY 2 9 1998	
JUL 2 8 1998	
OCT 2 3 1998	
MAY 2 7 1999	

DEMCO, INC. 38-2931

Protecting
Marie

Novels by Kevin Henkes

Protecting Marie

Words of Stone

The Zebra Wall

Two Under Par

Return to Sender

KEVIN HENKES

Protecting Marie

Greenwillow Books, New York

First Edition

1 2 3 4 5 6 7 8 9 10

This book is printed on acid-free paper.

Library of Congress Cataloging-in-Publication Data
Henkes, Kevin.
Protecting Marie / by Kevin Henkes.
p.   cm.
Summary: Relates twelve-year-old Fanny's love-hate
relationship with her father, a temperamental
artist, who has given Fanny a new dog.
ISBN 0-688-13958-2
[1. Fathers and daughters—Fiction.
2. Dogs—Fiction.]   I. Title.
PZ7.H389Pr   1995
[Fic]—dc20   94-16387   CIP   AC

For Laura

Contents

Part One

Without

1

❄

Fanny Swann popped the only red balloon, pretending that it was her father's heart. And then, within a matter of minutes, her anger dissolved into tears. After slapping at the remaining balloons, Fanny turned toward her mother, wrapping herself around her, burying her face in her mother's fancy dress.

"It's because of me," Fanny said between sniffles. "I know it's because of me."

"It's not because of you," Ellen Cross told her daughter. "Don't think that for another second." Ellen stroked Fanny's hair, pulling her fingers through it like a comb.

"I'm messing your dress," Fanny said, stepping away from her mother and wiping her nose on her sleeve.

"Don't worry about my dress."

"When will he come back?" Fanny asked, almost whispering. She looked at her mother up and down while she waited for an answer.

Usually her mother's long, thick, gray-streaked hair was drawn back into a ponytail that always managed to spill over her right shoulder and curve toward her neck. That night, Ellen's hair was twisted with a tinsel garland and small red berries into an elegant bun.

"Does it look stupid? Does it look like a Danish pastry?" Ellen had asked Fanny as she worked on her hair in the bathroom only hours earlier.

"It looks beautiful," Fanny had responded, her eyes frozen on her mother, mesmerized by her mother's ability to create extraordinary effects out of things that were nothing very special on their own. The tinsel garland was just a scrap that had been lying on the stairs; the berries were from a scraggly bush in the backyard.

Ellen's dress was satin. It was bloodred with flecks of yellow and green worked into the fabric here and there. The blending of the colors reminded Fanny of an apple turning. Her shoes were red also, with straps that buckled and heels that clicked on the bathroom floor.

"You look gorgeous," Fanny had said somewhat wistfully, as though she knew her mother's beauty could rub off on her daughter only by magic. Something Fanny did not believe in, except in books. "And you smell nice, too. What is it?"

"Oh, I'm not really sure. A little of this, a little of that."

"And add that to your already fragrant body odor," Fanny had joked, "and there you are—a masterpiece."

"*You* are the masterpiece. *You* are the perfect one."

"Right," Fanny had said sarcastically, jumping up to plant a kiss on her mother's cheek.

Catching glimpses of herself in the bathroom mirror as she watched her mother confirmed it all over again. Fanny looked a lot like her father. She often wondered why she had to resemble her father so strongly. Why not her mother? Fanny's features *were* her father's. They looked fine on him—a sixty-year-old man. They didn't on her—a twelve-year-old girl. Funny how a long nose with a bump, deep-set eyes, and a thickly furrowed brow can take on dramatically different qualities depending on whose face they happen to be part of.

Many of Fanny's parents' friends thought she was attractive. "You have a lovely Grecian profile," they'd comment. "Your eyes are so expressive, dear," they'd say. "You look pretty tonight, Fanny," they'd add. But all their flattery seemed false to Fanny. What did they know anyway? Many of her parents' friends were over fifty.

At school, Fanny felt extremely average. She did not belong to the popular clique. No one asked her for beauty tips in the lavatory. No boy had ever called her on the phone. And no one ever commented on her appearance, except for Bruce Rankin, who once said that Fanny Swann had a nose that could cut cheese.

Average. If you said it long enough, it sounded as bad as it felt. Average, average, average.

The one time Fanny mentioned her concern about her "averageness" to her father, he bristled.

"You are *not* average," Henry Swann stated, turning red. "It's your young, garbled vision clouding things. Hopefully, you'll outgrow it—your garbled vision. Then you'll see how beautiful you really are."

Her mother was more sympathetic, but just as blind.

Who's the one with garbled vision? Fanny often asked herself.

While Ellen had tucked in a few uncooperative strands of hair, Fanny had slipped in front of her and faced the mirror square-on. She straightened her outfit. She was wearing black tights, a black turtleneck, black Converse All-Star high-tops, and an old, brown, stretched-out, V-neck sweater of her father's, onto which she had randomly sewn dozens of buttons. The buttons were various sizes, shapes, and colors. I look like a clown, she thought. My mother is a goddess.

"Done!" Ellen had said, startling Fanny. She whirled about beneath the cool bathroom light like a dancer in a jewelry box.

Now they stood in the dining room, under the chandelier. Bright yellow balloons and green crepe-paper streamers hung down, moving slightly above their heads.

Ellen grabbed Fanny's hands and squeezed them tightly. Then she laced their fingers together. "I don't know when he'll be back. He didn't say. When he called, he just told me he wasn't coming to the party."

Fanny waited for her mother to say more. Things Fanny wanted to hear. Things like, "But I'm sure he'll be home soon," or "Surprise! It's just a joke—he's hiding in the front hall closet," or even something as simple and meaningless as "Don't worry."

But she didn't. She swung her arms out, making a circle with Fanny. The balloons bobbled in the small wind, and Fanny could hear the tight rubbery sound they made. And she realized that if the evening had turned out the way it had been planned, she would be hearing the laughter and talking and singing of guests celebrating her father's sixtieth birthday. By now, the room would be littered with crumpled paper napkins. Champagne glasses would be clinking. Half-eaten cocktail sandwiches and pieces of birthday cake would be sitting side by side on the huge pine table that had been pushed against the wall. Her father's colleagues and family friends would be scattered about in knots throughout the house. Instead, the house was empty, except for Fanny and Ellen holding on to each other, forming a ring in the dark.

"What are we supposed to do now?" Fanny asked, already playing out options in her mind: wait by the phone, call the police, hop in the car and start looking.

Ellen sighed and looked upward as if the ceiling held an answer. "I have this uncontrollable urge to do something that would annoy the hell out of him," she told Fanny. She puckered her lips and twisted her mouth into a funny shape. "I know," she said, "let's go to Burger King. I'm hungry, and I couldn't bear to eat those sandwiches or that cake."

"*Burger King?* Dressed like *that?*"

"I know, I know," Ellen said, her eyebrows raised. "It's the last place on earth I'd normally want to eat. And I wouldn't dream of going in this. But this is not a normal night. And just think how aggravated your father would be if he knew." Ellen squeezed her eyes shut for a long moment, and Fanny wondered if she were holding back tears.

"I'll turn on the answering machine," Fanny said. "And I'll leave a note on the table."

As she ran down the hallway to meet her mother at the front door, Fanny felt a burning in her stomach. She covered it up with her thick coat. She wound her scarf around and around her neck and pulled on her knitted wool cap and mittens.

Ellen jingled the car keys in one hand and smoothed

her coat with the other. "Let's go," she said. "Let's just see what happens."

It was a dense, moist December evening. The sky was purplish gray, and light. Fanny knew it would snow. She could almost hear it.

Fanny's ears were so sensitive that she had to have a fan running beside her bed every night, making white noise. If she didn't, she couldn't fall asleep. She'd hear the wooden floors creak, the refrigerator humming downstairs, the glass shrink and expand in the window frames. She could even hear the snow fall on the roof.

That night, there were many sounds. Small frozen puddles cracked under their feet, branches from the maple tree in the front yard scraped against the house, a dog howled in the distance, muffled voices traveled up chimneys with smoke. Fanny wondered if her mother heard any of it.

But once Fanny was buckled in Ellen's car, she became extremely focused; she didn't even notice the rattling of the engine or the gentle hissing of the heater. She was anticipating what her mother might say. And she was wondering if she would tell her mother what had happened that morning.

Neither spoke. Fanny listened so closely to her mother's breathing that she began breathing in the same rhythm. It was her mother's deep yoga breathing. In—

fill your lungs completely. Hold it. Exhale entirely. Push out every drop of air with your belly button. She knew her mother was trying to relax.

The Burger King was about a mile and a half from their house, and by the time they pulled into a parking space enormous flakes of snow were already twirling down.

Ellen rushed ahead to get inside where it was warm.

Fanny dawdled, watching snow land on her mittens and melt. "There's something I should tell you," she said softly. There, Fanny thought, I did it. She felt better having said even that much. But she also felt relieved that her mother was already opening the restaurant door and hadn't responded. Fanny ran to catch up. The entranceway floor was slippery, and Fanny slid into a man who was coming toward her on his way out. She grabbed for her mother's coat and held on to it as they walked to the counter.

Fanny wasn't very hungry, so she only ordered french fries and hot chocolate. Ellen ordered a Whopper, onion rings, and coffee.

Without hesitating, Ellen chose a booth near the side door. "I feel greasy already," she said. She took off her coat and plopped it down beside her. "And I feel perfectly out of place," she added, lightly running her hand over her hair.

Fanny pulled off her scarf, cap, and mittens. She decided to keep her coat on. It was saffron yellow with a large tawny stain across the back and a fake leopard-skin collar. Fanny had bought the coat at an antique store near school with her own money. Eight dollars. Her father hated it; she loved it. She was glad that the stain hadn't come out when Ellen had had it dry-cleaned. The stain looked like the head of a dog with pointy ears and its tongue hanging out. Fanny gathered the collar tighter around her neck. She breathed in its smell, and the fur tickled her nose.

"Well?" Ellen said.

Fanny dipped each end of a french fry into the pool of ketchup she'd made on a napkin. She bit off the ends, then dipped them into the ketchup again. After repeating the process several times, she was left pinching the tiniest piece between her fingers. She popped it into her mouth.

"What's the something?" Ellen asked.

"What?"

"You said, 'There's something I should tell you.' What's the something?" Steam rose from Ellen's coffee. She leaned over the cup and blew to cool it off. She blew and sipped, blew and sipped, while she waited patiently for Fanny to reply.

"I didn't think you heard me," Fanny said into her fur collar.

"What is it, sweetie?"

Fanny began stacking her mother's onion rings on a corner of the plastic serving tray. The tower rose—five, six, seven. And then it tilted. And then it toppled.

"You have to tell me, you know," Ellen said, nudging an onion ring.

A single tear squiggled down Fanny's hot cheek. "This morning," she said, "I ran up to Dad to give him a big birthday hug . . . and I was trying to be funny, I guess, or something stupid like that, and I said, 'Happy Birthday, Gramps.' I called him *Gramps*, Mom. And he hates me. And I know that's why he didn't come home for his party. . . ." Tears streamed into Fanny's hands. Her cheeks glistened. "I know that's why he left. Everything's my fault."

"Oh, sweetie," Ellen said. "*That's* why you were worrying?"

Fanny nodded and licked a tear.

"Come here," Ellen said, motioning with both hands. "Nothing's your fault. It's not like that at all. You could have called him Rip Van Winkle and it wouldn't have mattered."

There was a sudden burst of laughter from a nearby table. It made Fanny feel all the more regretful. She slid out of her side of the booth and joined her mother, scooching against her like she did when she was a baby.

"I know your father's having a hard time turning sixty. Forty wasn't tons of fun for me last year." Ellen dried Fanny's eyes with a napkin and draped her arm around Fanny's shoulders.

"But you seemed okay. You didn't do anything weird. Except eat half your cake. And devour cookies for two days straight." A small chuckle got tangled with a sob and Fanny coughed, as if something were lodged in her throat.

"Listen," Ellen said, "your father's worried about a lot right now. Retirement, having enough artwork for the show in New York, his health. The whole idea of growing old is scary. And a big birthday is so symbolic."

"What do you mean, his health?"

"I just mean he can't run or play racquetball every day like he used to. His knees bother him. His shoulder bothers him. When he *is* painting, his eyes grow tired and his hand goes numb. I think he's just concerned about . . . oh, I don't know, the future." Ellen glanced at her watch and twisted the band; then she looked straight at Fanny. "He just couldn't face having the party. And it's got nothing to do with you. Say it. Say, 'It's got nothing to do with me.' "

"Mother."

"Say it. It's . . . got . . . nothing . . ." Ellen prompted.

"It's got nothing to do with me," Fanny said weakly. A tightness squeezed her belly. "But is he okay? And where is he?"

"I think he'll be fine. It wouldn't surprise me if he went to the cabin." The bun of Ellen's Whopper looked as if a mouse had nibbled its way around the edges. All of a sudden she took a big bite. After swallowing hard, she said, "This tastes awful. Maybe I'm coming down with a cold—it feels like my mouth is crammed with flannel."

They ate silently for a while, pressed together at the far end of the booth. And then they both played with their food. Ellen kept thumping what was left of her Whopper with her pinkie, and Fanny was forming people out of the french fries and onion rings. The onion rings were perfect heads and the fries were arms and legs. She used ketchup to make them anatomically correct.

"You're sad *and* mad, aren't you?" Fanny asked, squirting ketchup all over an onion ring/french fry man that was running away from two onion ring/french fry women. Her eyes drifted up to meet her mother's.

Ellen nodded. "I'm kind of mad that I had to call everyone at the last minute and tell them that your father had the flu. But mostly I'm just sad that he's upset." Her voice grew quiet. "I know your father's difficult at times. But I know he loves you. Sometimes people have problems of their own that don't have anything to do with anyone else."

Fanny bit her bottom lip until it hurt. "Can we go home?" she asked.

"We'd better. Before they kick us out for being overdressed and for making such a mess."

"Maybe there's a message on the machine."

"Maybe."

"Maybe he's home."

When Ellen didn't reply, Fanny felt the sadness and anger all snarled up inside her more intensely than ever. Sad and mad, sad and mad, sad and mad, she said in her head like a chant as she cleaned off the table and dumped their garbage into a bin stamped THANK YOU.

The windows in the houses they passed on their way home were amber-colored and bright. Some of the houses were decorated on the outside with hundreds of small white lights strewn across shrubs and circling porch railings like stars. One had blinking lights framing the door like a chorus line of fireflies. With the snow falling, the street looked as perfect as the toy village beneath the Christmas tree at Fanny's house. When they drove by a house that was dark and seemingly empty, Fanny shivered. She hoped that when they pulled up in front of her own house it would be ablaze with lights, and that her father would be waiting—happy, talkative, and hungry for birthday cake.

2

❄

With only a few blocks to go before they reached home, Fanny played a game in her mind. If any of my father's initials are on the license plate of the next car we pass, he'll be home, she told herself. H. J. S.—Henry Joseph Swann. They drove by a sprawling brown Pontiac Catalina that was parked at a cockeyed angle and already collecting snow. Embossed in red on its license plate were the letters and numbers: KB 8207. "Damn," Fanny said under her breath. She pursed her lips and gave it two more tries before giving up. One car that came toward them had an F on its license plate, and Fanny wished that she had included her own initials in the rules of her game.

The roads were growing slick. Fanny could feel the car slide and shimmy. She sucked on her mittens, and the taste and smell reminded her of the old wooden bin by the front door that held enough gloves, scarves, hats, and mittens for five families. When they rounded the corner onto Forest Way, Fanny's street, the car fishtailed ever so slightly.

"I hope he's not driving," Ellen said, pumping the brakes. Her gloved hands glided across the steering wheel expertly.

Forest Way and two other streets, Whistler's Row and Lomond Place, formed a triangle. The streets created a border around a small tidy park. Young trees lined the park, and an assortment of squat bushes were clustered in each corner like groups of children. In the winter, the city parks and recreation department flooded the green to make an ice-skating rink. A street lamp stood tall at the far corner. It threw a perfect cone of light onto the rink, and because it was snowing the cone was speckled. Fanny would usually turn toward the park to see who, if anyone, was skating. But this night she craned her neck so that she'd see their house as soon as it came into view.

"Lights!" Fanny shouted, beating her wet mittens against her knees. "Yes!"

"But his car's not here," Ellen said calmly.

"It's probably in the garage," Fanny said. Her hand was already poised on the door handle, ready to pull it open the instant they reached the curb.

"Didn't *we* leave those lights on?" Ellen asked.

"Nope," Fanny answered, remembering how gloomy the house seemed when they had departed. "I turned on the porch light, but that's all." Excitement cracked her voice.

The house wasn't aglow, but the tiny bulbs on the Christmas tree twinkled through the window. And there was enough illumination from the floor lamp by the couch to cast blurry-edged rectangles onto the front yard. They fanned out toward the street.

Before Ellen had turned off the engine, Fanny was out of the car. She ran up to the house as fast as she could. *Plop, plop, plop.* As her feet hit the ground, little explosions of snow shot up, leaving huge footprints on the sidewalk as if a clown had just tramped by. Fanny noticed other footprints—her father's?—going to and from the porch, but she didn't pay much attention to them. She was hypnotized by the lights. The familiar tweedy smell of her father was nearly all she could think about. She could almost feel his arms around her as he welcomed her home with a hug.

After fumbling for her key, which she kept on a lanyard

around her neck, Fanny threw open the door and burst into the front hallway. "Dad!" she shouted. "Where are you?"

Silence filled the house, and Fanny knew immediately that her father was not at home. But he had been. He'd left the lights on. And he'd left gifts beneath the Christmas tree. Fanny glimpsed two small, wrapped boxes anchoring two monstrous, helium-filled balloons. Still, Fanny ran upstairs, checking every room to make sure. Not only could she smell her father, but she strongly sensed his presence. It was as if he had vanished mysteriously just seconds before she entered each room and a part of him still lingered. That eerie sensation heightened her disappointment. Then Fanny climbed up to the drafty attic that served as Henry's studio. Of course, it was dark and empty. If I had lights inside of me instead of bones and muscles, she thought, they'd all be going out. When Fanny came back down to the living room, Ellen was crouching by the Christmas tree. Her coat lay in a heap beside her.

"He's gone," Fanny said. "Here and gone."

"But he's okay," Ellen assured her. "He left a note. And he left these," she added, nodding toward the presents.

"What does it say?" Fanny asked.

Ellen handed an opened envelope to Fanny. Fanny unfolded the paper inside and read the note. It was written in Henry's elegant, slanted penmanship. It said:

19

Dear E. & F.,

I love you both more than ever. But I could not face a big party tonight. Please understand. I've gone to the cabin for the night. I just need to be alone. Traipsing through the woods by myself will do me good. Don't worry about me. I'll see you tomorrow night. We'll have a great Christmas this year. I promise.

Love,

Henry/Dad

P.S. Open the presents right away!

More to come!

"We should have stayed home," Fanny said. "Then he'd still be here."

"Don't think like that. And no, he wouldn't be—you know your father."

No one spoke for a few minutes until Fanny asked, "*Can* we? Open them right away? The presents, I mean."

"I guess," Ellen said. "Yes."

"You go first," Fanny said. "They're pretty, aren't they?"

"They really are." Ellen picked up the smaller of the two presents. Her name was written on a tag. The box was wrapped in gold foil paper and tied with silver ribbon. An abundance of loops and curls spilled over the box. Ellen untied the ribbon, and the balloon that was attached floated up to the ceiling. "You know, it's funny," Ellen said, eyeing the box, turning it in her hand. "I spent all day decorating the house, and it looks okay. Nice. And your father probably spent five minutes on these boxes, and they look gorgeous. The paper's perfect. The ribbon's perfect. And *his* balloons are helium filled." Ellen sighed and began unwrapping.

"It's kind of weird opening presents from Dad on *his* birthday," Fanny said as she watched her mother. Fanny took her coat, cap, scarf, and mittens off and used them as a cushion.

"Oh, boy," Ellen said, bringing one hand up to her mouth. "It's lovely. As always. Look."

Ellen held out a handsome brooch for Fanny to see. It was triangular with a raised, lacy network of roots patterning its entire surface. The lines were graceful, and it gleamed when Ellen lifted it up against her dress. "I'll bet Edward made it."

Edward Parish was a colleague of Henry's at the university. Edward taught metalsmithing. Henry taught drawing and painting.

"Let me put it on for you," Fanny said. She leaned forward and pinned the brooch onto Ellen's dress right where her heart would be. "It's beautiful," Fanny told her mother. She thought it made the gray streaks in her mother's hair look pearly and even more radiant than ever.

Ellen cocked her head downward, her chin pressing against the base of her neck. She patted the brooch. "Your turn," she said to Fanny, smiling.

First Fanny untied her balloon from her present, then tied it to her wrist. She ripped into her present like a child, her fingers working nimbly—tearing, tearing, tearing. The balloon jerked up and down.

Suddenly Fanny stopped. She had opened the box. She had seen what was inside.

"What is it?" Ellen asked.

Fanny handed the box to Ellen. "What does it mean?" Fanny wanted to know.

Ellen looked inside the box. She pulled out a glass statue of a dog. She examined the dog, examined the crushed tissue paper that was cascading out of the box. "I don't know what it means," she said in a quiet voice.

Fanny took the box, put the statue back in it, closed it, and shoved it as far into the corner behind the Christmas tree as she could.

"Do you want to talk about it?" Ellen asked.

Fanny shook her head no. She thought that she'd cry if they started to talk about dogs. "Can we make hot chocolate?"

"You bet. And how about some of that cake? I changed my mind—I don't care if it *does* say 'Happy Birthday, Henry' on it. It's too chocolaty and too thick with frosting to waste."

After making hot chocolate and cutting cake, Ellen built

a fire. They sat on the floor by the fireplace silently, eating and sipping, entranced by the flames. Periodically, Fanny would feel Ellen's hand on her shoulder, massaging it gently. Fanny loved the colors of a fire. The blues that flickered between the oranges like wings. And she loved the sounds of a fire, too. It sputtered and rolled and shot and roared. It crackled and splintered and spit. To keep her fingers warm, Fanny knitted them around her mug, or spread them wide, then flexed them right in front of the fire. She was mindful not to get too close, because her balloon was still tied to her wrist and she didn't want it to pop.

When they were done with their cake and hot chocolate, Fanny toyed with her balloon. She'd pat it and jab it, then pull it back to her. Then she'd pat it again. Over and over and over.

Ellen rose and reached up to retrieve her balloon. It was still hanging in the corner. She came back to Fanny and sat down. She untied the rubbery knot and pinched the rolled edges shut with her thumb and index finger. "I haven't done this in years," she said.

"Done what?" Fanny asked.

"This." Ellen brought the balloon up to her mouth and sucked in a mouthful of helium. She swallowed. "I love you," she said in a high cartoon voice. "I love you very much."

Fanny giggled and then laughed uncontrollably. "I've never done that," she said when she had calmed

23

down a bit. "I've heard about it, though. From kids at school."

"Here," Ellen said, handing the balloon to Fanny, sounding like so many Saturday morning animated characters.

Fanny inhaled, swallowed, and squeaked, "I love you right back. But I'm not so sure about my father right now." Somehow it was easier to say what she was thinking when her voice was so unreal, so comical.

It was Ellen's turn again. "I think the statue was just a well-intentioned bad choice." She passed the balloon back to Fanny.

Inhale, swallow. "Do you think it means he's bringing Nellie back home?" Fanny asked.

"No, honey," Ellen said firmly in her own voice. "Don't get your hopes up. Not even for a second. You know how much he hated having a puppy in the house." Ellen looked straight into Fanny's eyes. "Are you listening, Fan? I don't think your father would *ever* have another pet."

"No, Mom. Use this," Fanny said, pushing the balloon insistently at Ellen. "It's easier."

Ellen grabbed the balloon, but held it in her lap. She rubbed it like a crystal ball. "Do you want to sleep down here tonight? We can pull the futon out. Build an even bigger fire."

Fanny nodded. "And no more dog talk."

"No more dog talk. Come," Ellen said.

Fanny sat between Ellen's legs, her own legs crossed like a pretzel. They spoke to one another in thin, altered voices, saying silly, silly things until the balloon was flat and the fire needed to be stoked.

3

❄

Because she was so exhausted, Fanny fell asleep easily. But she had forgotten to bring her fan downstairs, and so she tumbled off the futon at about one A.M., nudged awake by the incessant sounds of the night. She heard a mousetrap snap in the basement. She heard the wind whooshing through the flue. She heard the radiator hiss and clank. But it was an eerie yelping sound that had jarred her awake completely, making it impossible to fall back asleep.

As she woke to the mournful noise, she was convinced

that it was Nellie, and her heart pounded with alarm. Only when she felt her mother beside her and made out the frame of the mantel in the bleary light, did she realize where she was and that Nellie was long gone. It had been months since Nellie had cried in the night, months since she'd been Fanny's dog.

Fanny padded across the living room floor as quietly as possible. She grabbed her coat on her way to the kitchen and tossed it over her shoulders like a cape. I must have been dreaming, she thought.

After turning the weak stove-top light on, Fanny heated water for tea. She used a regular saucepan rather than the tea kettle, because the kettle whistled shrilly and she didn't want to wake her mother. The tile floor was icy on Fanny's toes, so she hopped up onto the countertop while she waited for the water to boil. She swung her feet from side to side and back and forth.

When the water was ready, Fanny rinsed out her favorite mug and made strawberry tea in it. She had used it earlier for hot chocolate. The mug had been her favorite for as long as she could remember. Fanny didn't know who had given it to her. The mug was handmade, thrown on a wheel, the potter's illegible signature scratched sharply into the bottom. On one side, there was a kangaroo with a pointy joey peeking out of its pouch. On the other side, the words LOVE AND HAPPINESS were painted on in bouncy cursive writing.

Once when Henry was in a particularly cranky mood

and had been hounding Fanny about her table manners throughout the course of an entire dinner, Fanny held the mug up to him and said, "See, there's no father kangaroo. That's why it's my favorite cup. And that's why it says 'love and happiness.' " Then she stormed out of the dining room without having any dessert.

Fanny couldn't use the mug without thinking of that incident, and yet the mug remained her favorite even when she regarded Henry as the best father ever and her only champion in the world.

Right now, Fanny didn't know what she thought of her father. She knew that her mother was right: Henry wouldn't ever bring Nellie back. But the statue confused her. Her father was many things—particular, short-tempered, orderly—but he wasn't evil or mean-spirited. And yet, the statue seemed to be nothing more than a cruel reminder of the happiest time of Fanny's life.

Fanny hoisted herself back up onto the countertop. She pulled her knees against her chest for warmth and stretched her flannel nightgown so tightly over her legs that she could cover her feet completely with the ruffly trim. She stared into her tea, thinking about Nellie.

Fanny had wanted a dog all her life. Her best friend, Mary Dibble, always had a dog. In fact, sometimes the Dibbles had two or three, depending on which of the grown Dibble children were back at home, or if a stray happened by. It may have been at the Dibbles' that Fanny had first learned to love dogs, but it wasn't simply a case of seeing something your best friend has and wanting the same thing because that's what best friends do. Fanny sensed that from the moment she was born she was meant to have a dog. It was as though some unique and independent organ deep inside her, like a tiny heart, couldn't thrive properly without one.

Henry's resistance to owning a dog was just as strong as Fanny's desire. The more she pleaded for one, the more emphatic Henry's refusals became. He lectured her on the troublesome aspects of training a puppy, emphasizing how time-consuming and filthy the whole undertaking was. None of the sermons convinced Fanny of anything except how stubborn her father could be.

During an especially passionate discussion about getting a dog—which turned into an especially passionate discussion about responsibility and Fanny's allowance—in desperation, Fanny said, "And don't you know, dog is God spelled backward?"

Henry looked puzzled for a moment. Characteristically, he raised one eyebrow, shrugged, and said, "But I don't believe in God. You know that."

It finally got to the point where Fanny no longer confronted her father directly. But each year the words "a dog" appeared at the top of her Christmas list. And each year the words "a dog" appeared at the top of her birthday list. Fanny clipped dog cartoons from her parents' *New*

Yorker magazines and hung them on the refrigerator with magnets at Henry's eye level. Whenever Fanny bought a card for Henry, she made sure to find one with an image of a dog on it. Her personal favorites were those printed with William Wegman photographs.

Once, in a used bookstore, Fanny discovered a postcard of a reproduction of a Franz Marc painting. A smooth, creamy dog was lying in pure snow, its eye closed lazily, its paw slipped under its muzzle. Small shadowed dips in the snow encircled the dog. It took Fanny a minute to see them as hollows and not inky blue stones. The dog appeared to be so kind and lovable that Fanny thought, If an angel ever comes to earth as an animal, this is exactly the form it will take. At the time, the postcard had seemed like a charm, and just right for Henry's winter birthday, until days later when Fanny found it in the garbage, stained and saturated with wet coffee grounds.

For Henry's last birthday, his fifty-ninth, Fanny had Xeroxed a picture from one of the thick art history books that lined the bottom shelf of the bookcase in the living room. She'd decorated the image with colored pencils and glued it to a folded piece of construction paper. The painting she had chosen was Jan van Eyck's *Giovanni Arnolfini and His Wife.* Jan van Eyck was one of the painters Henry most admired. Fanny had picked this particular painting because there was a little dog standing as firmly as a chunky stool right in the middle of the foreground. The text in the book (most of which Fanny didn't understand) referred to the dog as an obvious symbol of faithfulness. On her homemade card, with a felt-tip pen, Fanny wrote, JAN VAN EYCK'S PORTRAIT OF ARNOLD FEENEY, THE FAITHFUL LITTLE DOG (HA!).

Henry never seemed to react to the cards and cartoons—he'd only raise one eyebrow the way he always did. But even Henry couldn't help but laugh at Arnold Feeney, and he tacked the card to the wall in his studio.

Although Fanny regularly kept up with her practice of clipping cartoons and buying and making cards with dogs on them, she had all but given up hope of ever having a dog of her own. And so, on the hot, hot afternoon last June that Henry came home toting a small wiggly bundle of bones and black fur, Fanny was completely stunned.

It was one of those moments in her life that she would never forget. She had been working in the garden in the front yard. Creeping charlie invaded the lawn and flower beds every year, and Henry paid her to keep the viney weeds under control. Fanny loved the mindlessness of the task and would have done it for free, but Henry offered her money, so she gladly took it. The temperature was in the nineties and the humidity was so high that Fanny wore only a bathing suit. She was kneeling on an old chair cushion, her dirty toes pushing against the soft, thick grass, when she heard her father's car round the corner a block away. She heard it pull up to the curb. She heard the door open and close. And then she heard the tiniest yelp. The tiniest, most lovely yelp.

When she turned and saw the puppy wriggling in Henry's arms, she trembled with joy. And she knew instantly by the way Henry looked at her that the puppy was hers.

Are you sure? she asked with her eyes.

Yes, he responded with his.

Everything froze. And Fanny trembled again. How long did everything remain still? Even the puppy was motionless. Perspiration dotted Henry's face and darkened his powder blue shirt. An overflowing basket hung from his shoulder. Fanny could see a rawhide chew-stick, a small furry football, red roses, and a bottle of champagne that reflected the sun and sparkled.

It was her mother's voice that made everything move again. *"Henry?"* Ellen called from the front door. "What's going on?"

Ellen ran down the porch steps and walkway toward Henry, and as she did she brushed against Fanny. When mother and daughter touched, Fanny's sense of time was altered again. Now, what she experienced seemed accelerated. She would remember only brief snatches that flitted rapidly. *Rat-a-tat-tat.* Fast, faster, faster.

She would remember her mother wiping her father's brow. And kissing him. "Are you sure you want to do this?" And, "New York?" And, "Oh, I love you."

She would remember her father's smile—curved and toothy. "I've had an incredible day." And, "Now we're four." And, "I think it'll be fine."

She would remember the zigzaggy and uncoordinated way the puppy raced to her. And how it licked the salty sweat off her legs. And how it settled into her lap and kept licking her, this time her face. She would remember how her hands encompassed its round, pink belly. And how warm it was. And how it was like the world. She would remember its smell—hot and loamy and sweet-stinky and comfortable. And how she knew it was female. And how she sang, "Smelly, smelly, smelly. Smelly, smelly . . . Nellie." And that was how the puppy got its name.

When things had settled down a bit and they were in the kitchen, Fanny learned why Henry was in such a good mood, why he had gotten the puppy.

"I had all but forgotten about sending the slides," Henry explained. "And so, when the gallery called the art office to say that they wanted to represent me, I was, well, elated. Understandably so." Henry laughed deeply and it sounded like pure bliss to Fanny. "I've lusted after this gallery for years."

"Will we get to go to New York?" Fanny asked.

"When they hang the solo show next year, we will."

Fanny watched her father closely. He gestured enthusiastically while he spoke, and his face seemed to be going through an extensive workout. The veins near his temples pulsed, his eyes widened and narrowed, his nostrils flared, and his muscles twitched. Henry was usually rather reserved, and he usually moved with great economy, as if there were nothing worse than a wasted word or an unnecessary action. But that day he hummed about the kitchen, opening and closing cabinets and drawers, punctuating his sentences by waving a champagne glass above his head, and kissing Ellen and Fanny every time he passed them.

"Once it sank in," Henry went on, "once I believed it all to be true and not a dream, I thought, This calls for champagne. And as I rushed to the car to drive to the liquor store I saw that little flower cart on the library mall. And so—two dozen long-stemmed red roses for you," he said, nodding to Ellen. "And right beside the flower cart, a shaggy student was stooped over a box of puppies. Free. He was giving them away. And so—a black, furry dream-come-true for you," he said, nodding to Fanny.

Henry's excitement was somewhat confusing to Fanny. He was represented by galleries in Chicago and Milwaukee. He had had galleries in New York and Boston in the past. His work had been reproduced in several books, and his shows had been favorably reviewed in *Art in America* and other magazines. But Fanny didn't question Henry. She just assumed that being represented by this particular gallery was a big deal. She had gotten a puppy as a result. Nothing else needed to be explained. Nothing else mattered.

Henry popped the cork on the champagne. They

toasted him. And they toasted Nellie. Last New Year's Eve when Fanny's parents had let her taste champagne for the first time, it had made her feel headachy, but now she drank it without hesitation, she was so happy. After swishing each sip around her mouth, she'd swallow slowly with her eyes closed, letting the bubbles tickle her throat.

She was sitting on the cool floor with her legs spread out in a V. Nellie rolled and tumbled in the small space Fanny had made. When Nellie tried to jump over Fanny's leg, she fell onto her back and waved her legs in the air like an overturned bug.

Henry and Fanny laughed. Ellen smiled.

Her mother suddenly seemed quiet to Fanny. Ellen set her glass down and began arranging the roses. The petals were so dark they looked black at the innermost whorl. "They're extravagant," Ellen said as she separated a few stems that were entwined and worked them into the vase. She tipped her head and arced it from one side to the other, admiring the flowers. As she rearranged a few of the roses, she pricked herself on one of the huge thorns. "Ouch," she said.

Henry came up behind her, turned her in his arms, and sucked her finger. "A small price to pay for all this happiness . . ."

"Yeah, Mom," Fanny said. She sprang from the floor with Nellie and came over to her mother and father. Nellie nuzzled against Fanny's shoulder, and Fanny nuzzled against her parents. Fanny echoed her father in a whisper, "A small price to pay for all this happiness . . ."

The first night she belonged to Fanny, Nellie cried. Fanny heard her and plucked her from her crate and took her to bed with her. As Fanny petted her and watched her relax and fall asleep, she knew that happiness was not exactly what she felt. This was better. She had never experienced this feeling before. For a moment she thought she might burst, and then as she drifted off to sleep, she felt enveloped by such warmth that she thought she might never wake up.

Raising a puppy was a lot of work, but Fanny was ready for it. And since it was summer, she had all day to devote to Nellie. Fanny's friend Mary Dibble helped. And so did Ellen, who used part of her vacation time from work to stay home to get Nellie off to a good start. Ellen was a book designer at the University of Wisconsin Press. For the first few days, Henry helped, too. He'd coax Nellie to the backyard so she wouldn't pee in the house. He'd walk her to the corner and back. He'd lie on the floor to give her ear massages. And he drove Fanny to the pet store to buy an immense sack of puppy food and several rubbery toys that whined when you squeezed them.

But then Nellie sneaked up to Henry's studio and peed on his Oriental rug. Twice. Nellie chewed on the legs of the dining room table. Nellie chewed on the legs of Henry's antique Cromwellian chair. Nellie had diarrhea all over the sun porch. Nellie continued to cry at night. Nellie growled at Henry and ran in circles about his feet. Nellie dug and dug and dug. Nellie nipped and nipped and nipped.

"They're just puppy things," said Fanny.

"I'm trying," said Henry. "I'm really trying. But look at my chair. It's irreplaceable. And it's ruined. And then there's my rug . . ."

"Please, don't yell at her *now*," said Fanny. "She won't understand."

"Damn it, she's tearing around the garden again," said Henry. "I will *not* eat lettuce that's been peed on."

"Give her a chance," said Fanny. "Please."

"Get her off the couch," said Henry. "Now!"

"I'm sorry," said Fanny. "But just because you had a bad day painting—"

"I don't want her running around under the porch," said Henry. "Good God, does she ever stop barking?"

"She's a *puppy*, Henry," said Ellen.

"I know," said Henry.

"He's your *father*, Fanny," said Ellen.

"I know," said Fanny.

"This isn't working," said Henry.

"She'll grow out of it," said Fanny.

"She's driving me crazy," said Henry.

"I'll die if you take her away," said Fanny.

"I can't paint at home anymore," said Henry.

"I thought this might happen," said Ellen.

Fanny threw a plastic cup against the wall. Henry slammed doors.

"I admit," said Henry, "I didn't know anything about dogs. Puppies. I thought that by now, by the time school started for you, that she'd be better. I thought that it would be fine for me to paint at home with her around on the days I don't teach. But I can't. I just can't. I can't get anything done when I'm home alone with her."

"It's not fair," cried Fanny. "This is the worst thing that's ever happened to me."

"I know, I know," said Ellen. "Of course I love her. But I love your father more. Adults make mistakes, too, you know. He's wrong, sweetie, but he's human. He made an awful mistake."

It was late August when Fanny wrote the ad for the newspaper:

> Free to a good home. Female black Lab mix.
> 4½ months old. Has shots. Is very sweet and
> friendly. Comes with toys.

The ad included Fanny's phone number. By listening carefully to the people who called, Fanny chose Nellie's new owners. They were a young couple who lived on a farm outside Madison. The night they came to pick her up, Fanny made a pile of all Nellie's belongings near the front door. She waited on the couch with Nellie curled up beside her. It was forbidden for Nellie to be on the couch, but Henry said nothing. Fanny had sobbed for so long that her eyes were sore and swollen.

"Will I ever see you again?" Fanny whispered.

Nellie sighed. Her tail curved into a sleek question mark.

Fanny liked the couple immediately—and Nellie seemed to like them, too. She scampered between the man and woman, sniffing their well-worn jeans and boots as if they held the most wonderful smells in the world.

The man wrote directions to their farm on a scrap of paper. "You can visit any time," he said. "Feel free."

"We'll keep the name," the woman said. "Nellie—it's nice."

Fanny watched them drive away in a pickup truck. Nellie sat on the woman's lap like a miniature child wearing a black cap with earflaps. For a moment, Fanny longed for the man to be her father.

Now, on this cold winter night, alone in the kitchen, thinking about Nellie and wondering what Henry could have meant by giving her the statue of the dog, Fanny grew angry again. She tiptoed to the living room to get her balloon. Then she took a piece of paper from beside the telephone and wrote, *At this very moment I don't understand my father and would like a new one. If you're interested, please reply.* Fanny wrote her initials and her address on the paper, tied the note to the ribbon that was attached to the balloon, and walked to the back door. She opened the door a crack and sniffed the cold air. Fanny stretched and poked her head out completely, keeping her feet as far inside as she could. Her toes were ice cubes.

It had stopped snowing, but the air was still thick, the sky still light. Although it was the middle of the night, it seemed like dawn to Fanny. All around, the sky was apricot colored; it peeked through the branches of the bare trees like fragments of stained glass. Everything appeared to be so peaceful outside. But nothing was peaceful inside Fanny.

Fanny hesitated for a moment, then let the balloon go. It wafted upward slowly, then got caught in a sudden gust of wind and was swept away quickly. Fanny watched the balloon without blinking. First it looked like a kite. Then it looked like two birds—one big, one small—far, far away. And then it looked like nothing at all but part of the mottled sky.

4

❄

The trees were heavy with snow; fist-sized clumps sat among the branches like white nests. Even the most slender twigs were marked with little pills of snow. Fanny stood at the window, squinting. She had known instantly when she woke up that she wasn't in her own room, because sunlight was pouring in through the windows. She could feel the heat on her face, feel the brightness make her eyelids flicker and hesitate. Her own room had only one small window and was in the rear, northwest corner of the house, where mornings were dull and dark in comparison to this.

Before Fanny had risen and stretched, she had reached out to touch the empty space beside her on the futon. It had been cold. She wondered how long her mother had been up. She wondered what time it had been when she, herself, had actually fallen back asleep last night after wandering about the house. And she wondered what time it was now.

As Fanny glanced out at the neighborhood, she realized that it had snowed several more inches since she had launched her balloon out the back door. If she remembered correctly, the trees had only been dusted with snow then. Fanny tilted her head and lifted her eyes. She searched the treetops and sky. The sky was a brilliant blue and endless. She almost had to laugh to herself—the idea of her balloon seemed silly now. Childish. Why did everything have such a different slant to it in the morning? Mornings were hopeful. Night— especially the deepest part of night after you awaken suddenly—seemed to intensify worries and troubles. Everything small became large. Everything bad became worse.

"Morning, sunshine," Ellen called. She emerged from the shadows of the dining room into the light of the living room, carrying a steaming mug of coffee. "Or should I say, sleepyhead?"

Fanny turned from the window with a start. "Morning," she answered in a froggy voice.

After setting her coffee down on the end table, Ellen gave Fanny a hug. Fanny noticed a sprinkling of white on her mother's maroon sweater. At first she thought it was snow.

"Oh," Ellen said, looking downward. "It's flour." She flicked it off as best she could. A faint halo remained.

"What time is it?" Fanny asked.

"About ten-thirty."

"I can't believe I slept so late," Fanny said. She was usually out of bed by seven o'clock, whether it was a school day or not. Fanny could tell that Ellen had been up for some time. She had showered; she was dressed; and she had washed her hair. Ellen's ponytail was shiny and smelled sweet, of almond shampoo.

"Help me move the futon back," Ellen said.

To the angry twang of springs extending and compressing, they pushed and pulled and maneuvered the frame back into its upright position.

"I hate that sound," Fanny said, flinching.

"I know."

"I always think something's going to snap and break."

"Me, too."

Ellen punched the futon into shape and scattered the throw pillows across it from armrest to armrest. Then Fanny and Ellen carried the coffee table back to its proper place, shoved the couch and chairs back, too. They folded the sheets and blankets they had used last night and piled them neatly with the pillows from their bedrooms on the stodgy corduroy chair.

Ellen grabbed her coffee from the end table and settled into one end of the couch. "Sit," she said.

Fanny yawned. She sank into the couch next to her mother, drawing her legs under her, leaning back on her heels. She yawned again. "That smells good," she said, meaning the coffee.

"Have some," Ellen offered, passing the mug to Fanny.

The coffee was hot, but not too hot, and it tasted wonderful. Ellen drank her coffee with a little bit of sugar and lots of cream. After several long, noisy sips, Fanny handed the mug back to Ellen. "How long have you been up?" she asked.

"Since about six-thirty."

"Six-thirty?"

Ellen nodded.

"I didn't keep you from doing what you wanted to do, did I?"

"No, no. Not at all. In fact, I took the birthday decorations down and I shoveled the front walk and I made cookie dough—as you can see." Ellen brushed her sweater again. "I wrapped a few presents, too. You," she said, smiling broadly, "were sleeping *so* soundly. I'm surprised you didn't wake earlier from all the racket I was making. I came to check on you several times. You were dead to the world."

Fanny shrugged. It seemed strange to Fanny that she could have slept through her mother's early morning bustling—the *whir* of the electric mixer, the *grrrrr* of the coffee grinder, the scrape of the shovel against the sidewalk—and yet, the tiniest whisper could keep her awake at night, cause her heart to pound until her heart itself pounded in her ears as loudly as a window slamming.

"Did anything else happen while I was asleep?" asked Fanny. "Did he . . . *any*thing?"

"No. Nothing."

"Oh," whispered Fanny.

"Well," said Ellen, "you must have needed it—your sleep."

"I guess." Fanny didn't feel like telling her mother about last night.

"The cookie dough is in the fridge. Why don't you get dressed and have something to eat? Then we can bake."

Fanny rose from the couch. "I'll be right down," she said. She started up the steps, then reached back and grabbed the newel post, facing Ellen. "What kind should we bake first?" she asked, kicking her leg out. Her foot was arched and her toes were pointed like a ballerina's. "Cutouts? Chocolate-chip drops? Or . . . rum balls?"

"Oh, Fan," Ellen said, "I'm only up for one kind. I

made dough for cutout cookies. I know you like them best." Ellen ran her finger around the rim of her mug. "We've got that huge cake anyway."

"Yeah," Fanny whispered, disappointed. Absently, she poked her toes through the spaces between the posts of the banister and picked at paint specks on the newel post with her fingernail. The wood was knotted and worn, and the distorted image of an old man's face that Fanny had discovered in the post when she was three years old suddenly transformed itself into a mosaic of Christmas cookies of every imaginable kind.

"You can bake whatever else you'd like," Ellen told Fanny. "I'm just not in the mood for more than cutouts this year."

"It's no fun to do alone. I wish Mary were here."

"Do you wish now that you'd gone with the Dibbles?"

Fanny shook her head no. She tried to muster up all the courage she had to shape this Christmas into a good one. She forced a smile.

Ellen looked at Fanny with such patience. "They'll be the best cutout cookies ever. I guarantee it. We'll go all out with decorating them."

"Okay," Fanny said, nodding. "Okay." She dashed upstairs to shower and dress.

Fanny had a lump in her throat. So much for her theory about mornings. She turned the water in the shower as hot as she could stand it. With her arms folded across her chest, she tipped her head back, then let it fall slowly forward until the water was beating against her neck. Water pooled at her elbows, and when she unfolded her arms to wash herself, the collected water hit the tile floor with a slap. She worked up a great lather all over her body. The bubbles contained little rainbows. She blew at them.

Why did Fanny feel so disappointed about baking only one kind of Christmas cookie this year? She and Ellen always baked far too many cookies. More than they and Henry could ever eat themselves or give away. A good number of them often turned stale, forgotten in the cupboard behind cereal boxes or the large tin of olive oil, until someone found them looking for something else and threw them out weeks, even months, after the holidays. But somehow Fanny felt that her world would only be right if she and her parents did all the same things for Christmas every year. And that included the number of kinds of cookies they baked. Starting at Thanksgiving, Fanny would look forward to Christmas with an odd combination of wistfulness and determination, long for it to be exactly the same as the perfect memories she held. (Had that perfect Christmas ever existed anyway?) Every detail had to be correct—from the cookies, to the village beneath the tree, to the fire in the fireplace, to the ham at three o'clock, glazed with honey and marmalade and trimmed with lettuce and spicy red gumdrops to look like holly.

❄   ❄   ❄

The Christmas Fanny was five, the weather had been balmy—sunny and in the sixties—unusual for winter in Wisconsin. Fanny sobbed. "This isn't the way it's supposed to be," she cried. "It's supposed to be snowy and cold. Like always."

Henry stifled a laugh and covered Fanny's small hands with his big ones.

Ellen brushed Fanny's long, damp bangs from her eyes. "Fanny," she said gently, "if you want everything to be perfect, you're just setting yourself up for disappointment. It doesn't always snow for Christmas—you know that. Why give yourself such a hard time, sweetie? It's Christmas—let yourself be happy."

Despite the heat, Fanny buttoned her dressy fur coat up to her chin, pulled on her mittens and brand-new ice skates, and sat on the front porch. Oh, how she wanted to try her new skates! But the rink, which should have been hard and smooth as a mirror, was a soggy brown puddle.

Determined as ever, Fanny stood, wobbling at first. She drew in a deep breath through her nose, and then she took off, stomping clumsily across the porch. She tried a figure eight. She tried to stand on one leg, leaning forward breathlessly. Mostly, she ended up grabbing for the porch railing, hand over hand, while her weak ankles caved in beneath her.

Fanny didn't realize how noisy she was being. And she didn't realize how badly she was scarring the soft pine floor until Henry and Ellen came out to see what the clatter was. Neither scolded Fanny, but the marks remained, and for months, if Fanny was in a particularly vulnerable mood and happened to pass the scarred floor, a wave of regret washed over her, making her hot.

I'm so stupid, Fanny said to herself. I'm not five anymore. But that's exactly how she felt. She wondered if she was the only twelve-year-old in the entire world who felt this way. Would a normal person her age even *care* about Christmas cookies? Or remember so clearly a Christmas so long ago? She watched a bubble rise from her hand. It bobbled as it floated upward. She imagined it growing larger, filling the shower stall, until Glinda the Good Witch of the East would come forth from the filmy shell in a sharp, quick *pop* to grant Fanny's every wish. To make everything perfect. Perfect cookies. Perfect Christmas. Perfect father.

When Fanny came back downstairs, she was flushed from her shower. The shirt she had on was an old one of Henry's. It was faded chalkboard green, flannel, and so worn that it was almost glossy under the fluorescent kitchen light. The elbows were threadbare, the stitching at the collar was loose, and the creases in the sleeves were white.

"God, I haven't seen that shirt in a long time," Ellen said. She casually held the old blond rolling pin in one hand as if it were no heavier than a twig.

"I took it out of a bag that Dad was giving to Goodwill a few weeks ago," Fanny said. The shirttail hung low over her jeans. She pulled on it with both hands.

"I loved that shirt. It's *so* soft." Ellen paused. "Your father looked good in it."

Fanny became acutely aware of how the shirt felt between her fingers. If she rubbed too hard, she thought it might disintegrate.

"Want some breakfast?" Ellen asked. "Before this becomes a full-fledged bakery?"

"I think I'll just pick at the dough. I'm not very hungry."

"Are you sure?"

Fanny nodded.

"Okay."

They smiled at each other for a long moment.

"I know you're thinking about him . . . as if you could help it," Ellen said quietly. "You know, there's no law against baking and talking at the same time."

Fanny shrugged and made a face.

Ellen blew a piece of her hair out of her eyes. "I thought I'd just open the door . . ." She spun the rolling pin, and it squeaked.

"Do you care if I quietly close it? The door. At least for now?"

"No."

"Thanks, Mom." Fanny pushed up her sleeves and playfully grabbed the rolling pin from Ellen. "I'm ready," she said. "To bake."

One pan of cookies—three long rows of stars, paper-thin—was already on the counter, just waiting to be popped into the oven. In what seemed to be a single effortless movement, Ellen picked up the cookie sheet, pivoted, opened the oven door, slipped the cookies in, closed the oven door, and set the timer. "There," she said as the cookie sheet shifted in the hot oven, making a muffled *clang*.

"How about angels next?" Fanny said. "Let's make lots of angels."

"Sounds good to me," said Ellen. "You can never have too many angels."

They baked angels and stars and bells and reindeer. They baked Santas and snowmen and trees. When they had begun working in the kitchen, the icicles outside the windows had been solid and thick. As the morning turned to afternoon and the kitchen filled with steamy heat, delicious smells, Christmas carols from the stereo, and stacks of golden cookies, the icicles melted. Fanny could hear the *drip, drip, drip* between songs. The windows had become misty, too.

As Ellen had promised, they went all out with decorating the cookies. They mixed five different colors of frosting. The frosting looked like stiff, chalky paint in the china bowls on the counter. Fanny dragged the step stool across the floor and scavenged in the cupboard. She found several dusty little bottles of decorations. Chocolate sprinkles and colored sugar made exotic angel robes. Cinnamon red-hots became the eyes of snowmen and the noses of reindeer. Nonpareils speckled bells and stars. Fanny saved the silver dragées for the angel wings.

Fanny arranged the completed angel cookies in a triangular formation on the table—some this way, some that way, each one precise in its placement—as if they were dolls. She stared at the angels until they appeared to be floating off the wooden surface en masse, hovering the way angels should. Do you call a group of angels a flock? she wondered.

There was a particular angel that caught Fanny's eye—it needed a few more dragées on its creamy white wing. Fanny touched it gently to see if the frosting had hardened. She thought the additional tiny silver balls would stick if she pressed them firmly into the frosting with her finger. This time when Fanny unscrewed the lid on the bottle, she noticed that the label on it said, NONEDIBLE. USE ONLY AS A DECORATION.

"Hey, Mom," Fanny said. "Look at this." She handed the bottle to Ellen. "We're not supposed to eat these."

Ellen read the label. As she turned the bottle in her hand, the shiny balls rattled, sounding like a maraca. "We probably shouldn't use them. I never knew they weren't meant to be eaten."

"*I've* eaten them before," Fanny said, her eyes widening with concern.

"I have, too," Ellen said. "Don't worry about it. Let's just throw them away." Ellen tossed the bottle into the garbage container under the sink. "Maybe we should pick them off the cookies. They'll look fine without them."

"They're just on the angels," Fanny said. "On the wings."

Ellen carefully plucked the dragées from each angel wing, and Fanny smoothed the frosting with a knife.

"They're not as pretty as before," Fanny remarked.

"Oh, well," said Ellen. "I think they look beautiful without them. Almost too beautiful to eat. *Almost.*" She picked up an angel from the table and bit its head off. "Mmm. This is very good," she mumbled. She offered the rest to Fanny.

Fanny broke off the wing. She ate it slowly, relishing every crumb. I'm eating the wing of an angel, she thought. The wing of an angel is inside me.

Just then, the telephone rang. Ellen answered it. The telephone was portable, and Ellen walked out of the kitchen.

Fanny stayed. She knew it was Henry. Her face tightened. She bit her lip. While she waited, she reached into the garbage container and retrieved the bottle of silver dragées. She didn't know why, but she wanted them badly. They were perfect little things. And she found it ironic that something so perfect and tiny and sparkly could be bad for you. She pushed the bottle into her pants pocket. Henry's shirt covered the bulge.

"That was your father," Ellen told Fanny from the doorway.

Fanny looked at Ellen expectantly.

"He said he'd be home by seven. And he said he was bringing dinner."

5

❄

Fanny waited for Henry in her room. She was organizing. Her thoughts, her room, her life. She had not inherited Henry's penchant for neatness, as a quick look around her room would clearly indicate. Schoolbooks lay here and there; two were turned over like sagging tents to hold her place. Scattered among the books were shoes. Shirtsleeves and tights snaked out from beneath the closet curtain. Drawers—opened ever so slightly, opened wide, closed—made the dresser look askew, tilting oddly forward.

When Fanny was younger, her messy room bothered Henry enough that he invented a game they would play once a week on the night before garbage day. It was called Stupid Hunt. "It's time for a Stupid Hunt," Henry would say, scooping Fanny up in his arms and marching off to her room. Bounce, bounce, bounce.

The first time, Fanny had been eager to participate, enchanted by the idea that her father had a secret game for the two of them to play.

"The object of our game," Henry had said, "is to look for stupid things. Things to throw away. And when we're done with our game, your room will be clean. How's that?"

Fanny shrugged, a bit perplexed.

"This looks like something stupid," Henry had said, picking up a wadded piece of lined notebook paper from the floor by Fanny's bed. "I think we should throw it away."

"No," Fanny had squeaked, instantly aware of the rules of the game. Instantly aware that Henry's game did not involve searching for pretend, dim-witted monsters or inept fairies, but rather real things—*her* things—things she wanted to keep. "You can't throw it away. It's part of my crumpled paper collection. Come see."

Fanny led Henry to her closet and drew back the curtain to reveal a messy pyramid of balled paper of all sorts and kinds piled into the corner and tumbling across the wooden floor. She thought that if Henry could see that the wad of paper had a place, belonged to a whole group of crumpled paper, of course he'd let her keep it. But he only wanted to dispose of the entire collection.

"How long have you been saving these?"

"Dunno." Fanny scrunched her toes. "They're families," she chirped.

"Families?"

"Uh-huh. The tissues are one family. The yellow paper's another. The white with blue lines is one, too. They all have lots and lots of children. No only children. And that's the queen. Her name's Marie." Fanny pointed to a doll that lay in shadow beside the lumps of paper.

Henry squatted and pulled the doll into the light by one of her legs.

"Careful," Fanny whispered, tugging on her collar. "She's very delicate."

And she was. Marie's torso and head had been cut from a Lucky Charms box. Her spindly arms and legs were thin strips of typing paper glued to the torso. The paper had been folded numerous times, accordian style, so that her arms and legs were springy. She looked as though she were dancing—one arm shooting upward, the other straight out, her legs forming an upside-down V. Fanny had drawn Marie's features with a black ballpoint pen. Her mouth was a pouty circle, and short, slitty lines served as eyes and eyelashes. She appeared to be winking. Marie had no nose, because Fanny already felt that her own nose was too big and therefore decided that a queen should have none. Her crown was a crinkly piece of aluminum foil stapled on at a funny angle, like a ship about to sail off her head. But the best thing about Marie was her royal dress. It was made of small paper scraps glued to her cardboard body. Fanny had used everything from wrapping paper to gum wrappers to newspaper. Of course, there were snippets to represent all of the paper families. In some places the glue was so thick you could see it through the paper. In other places Fanny had dotted the paper with beads of glue.

"Those are her pearls and diamonds," Fanny had explained, referring to the hard little globs, trying to point out all of Marie's special qualities. "Her heart is a tiny red balloon and her bones are really broken tea cups. But you can't see them. *Those* things are invisible."

"Can *you* see them?" Henry had asked, his eyes twinkling. He held Marie up and blew at her legs. They quivered.

"I don't have to. I just know they're there."

"Hmm." Henry handed Marie to Fanny. He tipped his head and rested his index finger at the corner of his mouth. Then he stroked his face thoughtfully. "Well, I suppose Marie will survive this Stupid Hunt, but most of your wads of paper have to go. Your room's a firetrap. It will be as neat as a pin when we're done. You'll like it. You'll see." The tone of Henry's voice seemed to say, I know everything there is to know about anything that matters.

But Fanny did not like it. Her room looked empty, less comfortable, sad even. By the time the Stupid Hunt was over, Henry had filled a paper bag with well over half of Fanny's crumpled paper collection, four used tissues from under her bed, a napkin, twelve wilted dandelions, several twigs, a clump of creeping charlie, an empty ginger ale can, a scraggly bow from a birthday gift, a pen cap, two broken rubber bands, and a piece of a stale cookie.

There was a reason why Fanny needed each of these things, but she knew her father could not be persuaded to change his mind. As she had watched Henry fill the bag with her belongings, she had clutched Marie firmly to her chest, risking bending her. She was grateful that when Henry had clapped his hands and said, "Finished!," Marie was still in her arms.

That night, before bed, Henry, Ellen, and Fanny had ice cream on the screened back porch. It was a muggy night, with only a slight, seldom breeze. Bugs flitted against the screen, drawn by the overhead light. Henry let Fanny pour her own chocolate sauce, and she rewarded herself with an abundance of it. She felt she deserved it. Because the ice cream was melting so quickly, Fanny stirred it and ate it like soup. The bowl sweated. Water dripped onto her nightgown. Henry praised Fanny to Ellen and called her Fancy and Fan-fan—his pet names for her that he only used on rare, special occasions. But Fanny barely heard; she was already anticipating the next

Stupid Hunt, trying to figure out a way to protect Marie, certain that Henry would look for her, find her, and throw her away.

The Stupid Hunts went on for months. Each week Fanny found a place to hide Marie. And each week Marie survived.

Had it only been in Fanny's mind that Henry had been hell-bent about getting rid of Marie? A complete misconception? An overactive imagination at work?

Now, at age twelve, Fanny had long outgrown Stupid Hunts and Marie. She simply kept her door closed, her messy room hidden from Henry. And Henry rarely entered her room anymore, and when he did, he generally refrained from commenting, although a few times Fanny had noticed him glance around and roll his eyes before leaving.

Fanny still had Marie. She didn't think about her much; she did, however, know exactly where she was. Marie had her place. It was the back left-hand corner of the bottom drawer in the white file cabinet that stood near Fanny's dresser. Henry had given the file cabinet to Fanny when he had bought a new one for his studio. Fanny had nothing to file, per se, so she used the file cabinet as a secure home for her most prized possessions. The cabinet drawers locked. Originally, this fascinated Fanny, because she had never owned anything like this before, never had the chance to be secretive in this way. There was no lock on her bedroom door, no lock on her jewelry box. Once, after receiving the file cabinet, it occurred to Fanny that having it during the days of the Stupid Hunts would have been a perfect solution to her problem. She could have placed Marie, or anything else she was worried about losing to Henry, in the cabinet and turned the key, guaranteeing safety. It would have been as simple as that.

The key to the cabinet clinked against Fanny's house key as she kneeled and pulled them out from under her shirt. She had worn both keys around her neck for years. The house key was solid and heavy and golden. The key to the file cabinet was thin and silver and nearly weightless. Fanny opened the bottom drawer. She laid the bottle of silver dragées down right next to Marie.

The file cabinet was filled with many beloved things: three shells Fanny had found when she went to Martha's Vineyard with her parents one summer; a translucent handkerchief stitched with rows of leafy daisies that had once belonged to Grandmere, Henry's mother; a Christmas stamp from England, torn from an envelope, of a snowman looking at a child through a window; a black-and-white photograph of Henry as a boy riding a tricycle; a color photograph of Ellen as a girl drowning in a wave of Oriental poppies; three ribbons—one red, two white—that Fanny had won at a summer track meet for children at the university; and a sketch of Fanny, an infant, curled up with her fists at her mouth like a kitten, drawn by Henry.

There were smooth stones from their cabin in the

woods, a multicolored beaded necklace Ellen had worn to her high school prom, and a bicentennial quarter. There was a brittle maple leaf crown Ellen had woven for Fanny's last birthday. And there was the small slip of paper on which were written directions to the farm where Nellie now lived. Fanny had unfolded and folded the paper so many times it was beginning to fall apart at the creases. She wondered if she'd ever have the courage to visit Nellie. She wanted to, and she didn't. She thought she would; she knew she couldn't.

Before closing and locking the drawers, Fanny gingerly removed Marie. Marie was swaddled in a sheet of tissue paper so thin Fanny could see Marie through it as if she were embedded in ice. Fanny unwrapped her. The doll seemed so small and flimsy now. Her arms and legs were folded in against her body like the petals of a flower. Fanny peeled them away. "Will it be a merry Christmas?" she asked Marie.

Marie lay in Fanny's hand, still and silent.

"That's exactly what I was thinking," said Fanny. She bundled Marie up, placed her back in the file cabinet, and closed the drawer with a *rmm-click*.

While Fanny straightened her room, she could hear the linen closet door open and slam shut. Again. Again. She could hear Ellen walk heavily across the floor. She could hear the floor creak and hangers clatter against one another and ring. Fanny knew that her mother was organizing, too. They were both killing time, waiting for Henry. Like mother, like daughter. Frowning, Fanny decided to quit. She would leave her dresser drawers open. She would leave her dirty socks on the throw rug. She plunked herself down on her unmade bed defiantly and rested her eyes. Within minutes, her whole body yawned, she was so drowsy. Spots swam beneath her eyelids. She tightened and relaxed her eyelids, and the spots pulsed like flames.

As she was drifting off, Ellen's voice kept replaying in Fanny's head: "Scratch the surface of anyone and you're bound to find complexities." And "Secondhand pain is the hardest to deal with." Ellen had said these things to Fanny while they had been cleaning up the kitchen after baking cookies. The remarks had come right out of the blue. The remarks, Fanny knew, referred to Henry, but she didn't quite understand them. Was her mother trying to explain Henry? Rationalize his behavior? And her father wasn't the only one dealing with pain. Or maybe that's what "secondhand pain" meant—that Ellen and Fanny were feeling pain, too, because of Henry, and that theirs was worse.

Fanny didn't know. It all confused her. She did know, however, that what her parents did or how they felt had a strong effect on her. If Henry, for example, was in a grouchy mood—not to mention skipping his sixtieth birthday party and staying away for the night—it cast a shadow over everything. It occurred to Fanny that children, as they grow older, probably forget how awful it is to experience that powerlessness; if they didn't, they would never have children of their own. They'd be too afraid of the influence they'd have.

Sometimes Fanny wondered if *she* would have children. Sometimes she thought that having a baby to take care of would be wonderful. She loved playing with Mary Dibble's three-year-old brother, Joey. Since she had no siblings of her own, she had taken a special interest in Joey—sending him origami birds in colored envelopes through the mail, hiding small bags of candy in his room, phoning the Dibbles and asking for Batman, his latest obsession and dual identity. He had just begun to call her Auntie Fanny, having been prompted to do so by Mary. Whenever he said it in his high, tittery voice, Fanny felt a rush of pride.

The mattress squeaked as Fanny turned over. She lay on her side, her head on her flattened hands, her legs bent. After a deep sigh, she fell asleep thinking of Joey and Mary and Christmas and presents and snow and skating in circles and circles and circles....

"Fanny?"
Knock, knock, knock.
"Fanny?" The door opened, Ellen peeked in, and a

triangle of light bleached the floor. "Fanny, telephone," Ellen said, approaching the bed.

Fanny yawned and sat up. "Is it Dad?" she asked.

"No, it's Mary. She's calling from Florida. Here." Ellen handed the portable phone to Fanny and quietly walked out of the room.

"Mary?"

"Fan, hi," said Mary Dibble. "I miss you."

"Me, too."

"I'm having the worst time. I wish you had come with us."

It had been such a difficult decision for Fanny to make. Part of her had wanted to go with the Dibbles. But a bigger, stronger part of her couldn't bear to be away from her parents for Christmas. She had agonized for a week in October, straining to picture it both ways in her mind. And then there was her father's birthday. That's the excuse Fanny finally used; she told Mary that it was because of Henry's sixtieth birthday, and the party they would surely have, that she felt she couldn't go.

Both Ellen and Henry had given their approval freely, almost pushed Fanny to go. "You'll have fun," said Ellen. "It's kind of exotic to have Christmas in a warm place," said Henry. If only they had said no, it all would have been so easy. She wouldn't have had to decide. She could have told Mary the simple truth and then pretended that she was furious with her parents.

Fanny knew that if she had gone, she would have been homesick. She might have gotten a tan, but she would have had to endure a lump in her throat the size of a plum the entire trip.

"It's not so great here, either," said Fanny. She paused and rolled her tongue. "My dad didn't show up for his party."

"Why?"

"I'm not sure. My mom says it's because he's afraid of turning sixty, or something. I don't know." Fanny didn't want to say more than that. Talking on the telephone was a poor substitute for having a conversation face-to-face. Mary would hear everything when she came home. "Do you have a tan yet?"

"Try a burn. I'm kind of pink all over. I fell asleep outside at my grandma's. I hope I look normal by the time we come back."

"You'll still look better than me," Fanny said, glancing at her left hand. She wiggled her fingers and waltzed her hand back and forth. "A winter ghost, as usual. Hey, how's Joey?"

"He cried at Disney World. Tom scared him silly. I think fourteen-year-old brothers are a curse. Get this: He convinced Joey that it wasn't called Disney *World*, but Disney *Worm*, and that invisible worms were every-where—falling from buildings, coming up through the ground, even streaming out of Mickey Mouse's ears and eyes."

"Tom's a creep."

"Tell me."

"Was Joey okay?"

"After about a half hour of comforting from my mom, he was all right, I guess. But he kept scratching himself, and Tom would blow on the back of his neck or touch him with a stick or something, and he'd jump like a rabbit and shriek, 'Worms! Worms! Go away!' It was great, though—my dad called Tom a worm for two whole days and swatted him, too."

"Poor Joey."

"He was *so* cute, Fan. I tried to explain how many miles away from home we were, and all he kept saying was, 'A mile is when you take a trip. A mile is when you take a trip.'"

"Give him a big fat kiss for me."

"I will. I think we're the only normal ones," said Mary. Her lips made a funny sound. "I think I hate my family. Especially Billy and Tom. You couldn't ask for two worse brothers. They're fighting all the time and driving my mom crazy. And my dad bought this pair of shorts with Donald Duck heads all over them, which he actually wears in public."

Fanny giggled. She could picture Mr. Dibble wearing his shorts with pride. Not one ounce of embarrassment. That's what she liked about him. He did things her father would *never* do.

"I keep thinking," Mary continued, "with my luck, I'll

run into some cute guy when I'm with him, and I'll have to say that the goofy man in the kiddie shorts is just some harmless weirdo who's been following me around."

After Fanny laughed, there was a staticky silence.

Mary's voice changed. "And then there's my grandma. A really strange thing happened."

"What?"

Mary sighed. "Well . . ."

Waiting, waiting.

"Mary, what happened?"

"Well . . . I walked into the bathroom at my grandma's in the middle of the night. Last night. From the hallway I could see the light shining under the door, but I didn't think anyone was inside because she *always* leaves the light on. So I opened the door and—bam—was face-to-face with my grandma. She was just leaving. She startled me completely, but more than that, she looked so . . . *scary*. Her hair was long and stringy and hanging all over her shoulders. Down to her *waist*, like an octopus or something. I didn't even know it was her at first. I've only seen her with her hair in a tight, neat little bun. That's the way it's been all my life. I never even thought about her *having* long hair before." Mary paused. "I was shaking all over for a second. She didn't know I was so upset. At least, I don't think she did. She just kissed me on the forehead and shuffled out of the bathroom. She didn't mention it today."

"You're not scared now, are you?"

"No. Now I feel stupid. But I'll never think of my grandma in the same way again. I know it shouldn't have, but it really freaked me out." Mary breathed deeply and exhaled right into the receiver. "I was so upset I broke our promise about our gifts to each other, about waiting for Christmas. I opened mine at about two A.M. *And*—I loved the earrings. And so you have to open yours. Right now. While we're on the phone. I'm wearing them as we speak, you know. I look smashing."

"Let me get it," said Fanny.

The gift from Mary was on top of Fanny's dresser. It was a small box, wrapped in a cover torn from a *Seventeen* magazine. Fanny ripped the paper, opened the box, and laughed. "Can you believe it?" she said. "You have excellent taste."

"And so do you."

They had given each other the same earrings. The earrings were simple, but beautiful. Each one consisted of three clear, marble-sized beads dangling from a silver hook. The beads had wavy threads of orange running through them. They looked like pieces of hard candy.

"I got them from that vendor on State Street," said Fanny. "You know, the woman with the huge pink cheeks and the weepy eyes. The one who wears patchouli."

"Me, too."

"Of course."

"Of course."

"I can't believe we bought the same exact earrings," said Fanny.

"Maybe it's a sign."

"Of what?"

"Maybe it means we're really sisters," said Mary. "Oh, oh—I'd better hang up. I hear someone coming, and I'm using my dad's calling card. He'll kill me sooner or later, but I'd rather it be later. Bye."

"Bye."

Click. Bzzzzz.

The round green light on the phone went out when Fanny tapped the button that said TALK–OFF. She set the phone down on her bed and turned to face her mirror. The oval mirror was framed in gold and hung above her dresser, leaning slightly to the right. Before she put her earrings on, she pushed her nose up with her index finger. If only my nose were a bit smaller, I'd be pretty, she thought.

One earring got tangled in a strand of hair as Fanny tried to fasten it. When they were both in place, she tossed her head. With each movement she made from side to side, the beads produced a fine, thin sound.

Fanny stopped; the earrings stilled. She studied herself in the mirror. She tried to imagine what her face would look like when she was an old woman. She wondered how old she would be when *she* would begin to scare children simply because of her appearance. Her face registered a momentary surge of sadness for Mary's grandmother, and then it occurred to her that one day soon her father might find himself in a similar situation. One day soon he might frighten someone. All of a sudden, Fanny breathed on the mirror, and her image disappeared in a fog. She moved away from the mirror, turned her back to it. She just wanted everyone home. Everyone, meaning her father and Mary.

Before she left her room to find her mother, Fanny made her bed. Then she closed her eyes and touched both earrings at the same time. "I wonder where he is this very minute," she said to no one at all.

Part Two

With

6

❄

Listening. Listening. Listening. Watching the clock. Listening. Listening. Listening. Fanny's ears pricked up at the dull thud of a car door slamming and footsteps on the porch. Interspersed with those familiar noises was a soft, sharp ringing sound. What is *that?* she asked herself. If she were still a little girl, she would have been convinced that it was reindeer bells or the secret language of Christmas elves. Determined to act nonchalant, Fanny stayed upstairs. I'll wait until I'm called, she thought. This meant she had to fight with herself to stay put. The urge to race down the steps to greet her father at the door was so powerful she had to grasp the banister tightly, bite the inside of her cheek, and will her feet to behave like rocks.

Amid the rustlings of coming home, Henry's voice resounded. "Fanny! Oh, Fancy!" At the same time, the hallway clock marked the hour and Fanny took the steps two by two.

Dinner and Henry arrived at seven o'clock sharp, just as Henry had said. Dinner was not what Fanny had expected. Dinner was a dog.

Fanny saw her father and brightened immediately. And then she saw the dog. Her heart leaped, but fluttered and fell just as quickly. It was amazing how this moment reminded her so of the moment she had first set her eyes on Nellie. Nellie. The beautiful, black, shiny puppy that had been hers and no one else's.

"Whose is he?" Fanny asked.

"He's a she," Henry replied. He released the dog from its leash, but the dog remained still as stone until Henry said, "Okay."

The dog swept through the living room and stopped right at Fanny's feet. The dog sat. Wet pawprints connected Fanny to Henry like the links of a chain.

Then Henry walked over to Fanny. His coat was still on, and his hair had been whipped into a frenzy by the wind. He stood at her side. Father, daughter, and dog became the three points of a triangle. "Fanny," said Henry, "I'd like you to meet Dinner. Dinner, my daughter, Fanny. You belong to each other."

Something stirred inside Fanny. *"Dinner?"* she said to Henry.

"Yes, Dinner. I know it's an odd name, but she's had it for three years, so I think she's stuck with it."

Dinner straightened, making herself very tall; then she cocked her head ever so slowly. All the while, her big, round eyes were blinking. They were the brown of root beer with glassy black pupils. A dot of reflected light, like a spark, gleamed in the middle of each pupil. A circle in a circle in a circle. Two little targets.

Fanny didn't know where to look. If her eyes rested on Dinner for more than five seconds, she was afraid she'd be taken with her. If she looked at Henry, she was afraid she'd forgive him. She stared at the bowl of pinecones on the coffee table.

"Well," said Henry, "Merry Christmas. A few days early."

What was she supposed to say? Or do? It struck Fanny that she hadn't even hugged her father yet. She swayed, and steadied herself by reaching out to him and grabbing onto his coat. She kept her eyes glued to the bowl of pinecones; it blurred into a brown cloud.

"Merry Christmas," Henry murmured again. He embraced her tightly, squeezing her shoulders with his fingertips. Her face was mashed against his navy blue scarf, and she could smell smoke from the wood stove at the cabin. After they had broken away from each other, Henry ran his hand along her cheek, as if he were trying to absorb all her doubts. "It's for real this time," he told her. "I promise."

Be intrepid, Fanny told herself. Intrepid. It was a word that Henry had taught her, a word that meant unshaken, dauntless. To be intrepid, Henry had said, was admirable. Fanny swallowed. "May I have that in writing?" she asked slowly. She was surprised at the sureness of her voice.

Twice, Henry's eyebrow rose and dropped. "Don't you trust me?" he asked. But before Fanny could respond, he added, "You don't have to answer that."

Be intrepid. "*May* I? Have it in writing?"

"Have I ever asked you for a contract? For you to write something like this down?"

"You don't have to," Fanny whispered. "You're the parent. I'm just the kid."

Their eyes connected, and Fanny almost smiled a nervous smile.

"Listen," said Henry. He dragged his hand through his hair, then pointed to the couch. "Sit for a minute." As Henry lowered himself to sit, his coat bunched up around his waist in thick folds, making him appear overweight. There was a weariness to his voice, and the lines beneath his eyes and those that stretched to his ears seemed sharper and deeper. "Where to begin . . ." said Henry.

Fanny shivered. All of a sudden, her toes were cold. She flexed them inside her clunky boots, trying to warm them up.

"Nice shirt," said Henry.

Fanny shrugged. Now, she wished that she wasn't wearing her father's old shirt. She was playing with a loose button. It was tortoiseshell. Loops of thread formed an X that kept the button in place, but just barely. Fanny turned the button as far as it would go in one direction, then turned it back.

"Soft as chamois," Henry remarked. Absently, he rubbed his fingers together as if he held the shirt between them. "It's strange how some things happen at the same time—the birthday thing and Dinner—as if there were some freak law of nature causing it. Anyway . . ." he said, then licked his lips. "There's a lot I could say, but for now this will suffice: I'm not going to discuss whether I was right or wrong about last night, but I was wrong before. There was no possible way for me to live in the same house with Nellie, but I know that giving her away undid you. And that undid me. It's really been getting to me lately, and, well, with Christmas . . ." Henry crossed his arms against his chest and leaned back into the cushions. "Feelings are so complicated. They run so deep and go so far back. I know you've been upset with me for months. When you were little, my shortcomings were small enough that all I needed to do to be forgiven was to tickle your toes or plant kisses behind your ears or give you a glass of milk with a piece of red licorice to use as a straw. It's not that easy anymore."

Fanny's mouth became an O. She felt a small tremor of recognition. "You remember that?" she asked.

"What?"

"Milk with licorice. I'd forgotten all about it."

"Of course I remember. I remember more than you think."

It only took Fanny a matter of seconds to recall how her fingers would circle the glass of milk, her head bent over it in anticipation. Then, using the licorice as a straw, she would sip the milk and blow bubbles into it. Soon the milk would taste faintly of cherries and turn a dusky shade of pink. "Red licorice," said Fanny vaguely.

The dog had inched her way over to the couch. She plopped her head down between Henry and Fanny. Give me some attention, please, was the message her moony eyes seemed to be sending.

"Lie down," Henry commanded, and immediately Dinner's head disappeared with a doleful sigh and the rattle of her tags. Henry sighed, too, and Fanny couldn't tell if he was imitating Dinner or not. He took one of Fanny's hands and sandwiched it between his. "I couldn't begin to count how many times I've kissed your little fingers, your little nose, your little toes. I hope somehow you're aware of that, even when you're doubting me." His voice was perfectly even. "Your toes used to be pudgy and pale like white jelly beans." Henry nodded toward Dinner, then leaned closer to Fanny. "And *her* toes are hairy and wet and somewhat stinky. But she's yours." He paused. A long, lingering pause. "That is, if you want her. . . ."

The magnitude of the situation was becoming clearer and clearer to Fanny. My whole life could be changing right before my very eyes, she thought. While she considered how to answer her father, she had to remind herself to breathe.

"Henry, we need to talk," Ellen said, suddenly and simply. It seemed as if she had materialized out of nowhere. She was standing in dim light near the front door, holding two bags from Burger King and a bottle of wine. On the floor, a shopping bag teeming with parcels rose up to her knees like a small, sturdy house. Snow dusted her shoes and clung to her hair. Fanny hadn't noticed her until she spoke, and she was curious as to how long her mother had been waiting there.

Had her parents said *anything* to each other yet? Had they kissed? She must have met him at the door, then gone out to the car to retrieve the bags, Fanny reasoned. She probably knows as little as I do.

Ellen moved across the room purposefully, the bags

clutched tightly in one hand, the bottle of wine propped under her arm. With her free hand she grasped Henry's sleeve and led him away.

Fanny watched as Henry and Ellen walked to the kitchen. She thought that her father had never looked older and that her mother had never looked younger. Usually, they just looked like her parents.

Fanny followed her parents. And Dinner followed Fanny. The two of them only made it as far as the swinging door that separated the kitchen from the dining room. It was nearly always open (unless they had company); now it was closed. The creaky door was still swaying slightly on its rusty hinges, until Fanny stopped it with her shoulder. She slid down against the door, down to the floor, and extended her legs before her, straight as yardsticks. Dinner squeezed between Fanny's legs, shoving them as far apart as they would go, then turned onto her back, her belly pushed forward and upward, prominent as a roasted turkey.

"Okay, I'll scratch you," Fanny whispered. "But only for a minute. And I can't really look at you or get to know you—yet. Not until I know it's safe."

Dinner stretched and made a long, high, moany sound that ended in a short bark.

"Shhh," Fanny uttered faintly. "Let's listen."

From behind the door, voices lifted and dropped, then became soft whispers—soft, *fierce* whispers. There were brief silences before they started up again, and during the absence of voices Fanny could hear plates and silverware being placed onto the table, keys being fiddled with, a napkin ring rolling across the counter, tap water running.

Fanny knew that her mother was collecting details, the pieces of the puzzle that had taken Henry away from them and returned him with a big, friendly dog.

Intermittently, the voices were clear. Ellen said, "But you're an adult! Imagine how confusing it must be for a twelve-year-old." Later, she said, "I don't care what other people think," and "Maybe you should see someone." Most of the time, Henry was mumbling in a low tone that Fanny couldn't understand at all, except when he'd say, "Damn it," which he did several times.

"Who cares?" said Fanny. Finally, trying to drown it all out, she singsonged, "La-la-la-la-la-la ..."

Dinner's ears perked. One stood erect and the other shot off to the side, the tip curled over. The insides of her ears were pearly and pink with ridges and knobs that swirled into darkness. They reminded Fanny of seashells. She rested her ear against Dinner's and listened for the ocean.

Eating a piping hot Whopper and french fries at Burger King is one thing; eating a Whopper and fries that have grown cold on a winter night and been reheated in an oven at home is entirely another. The tomato slices and soggy lettuce leaves were especially unappetizing, even for a diehard fan. Using real china didn't help one bit. Fanny was amazed, however, at how much of the food her parents were eating.

Both of her parents were subdued, and their faces showed traces of postargument stress—tight cheeks, sharp eyes, flushed skin. Fanny hoped that her father would tell her all about Dinner. But no one said much of anything.

Dinner was lying on the throw rug in the corner, close to the warmth of the oven. With her front legs crossed directly above her paws and her head held firm and even, there was a strange and humorous air of elegance surrounding her. Because of it, her collar and tags took on the appearance of flashy adornments.

Fanny hid her head and stifled a laugh. The stiffness that had descended upon the kitchen, overwhelming them, made it seem wrong to giggle, much less laugh. But holding it in was a difficult task. Each time Fanny glanced at Dinner, it struck her more deeply how comical she looked.

"Who does she think she is, Catherine Deneuve?" Ellen said, her voice bubbling. She had barely managed to get the words out before she burst into a lovely fit of laughter. Mockingly, she flipped one wrist over the other and barked once.

Now Fanny felt free to laugh, and so she did. Henry did, too.

Ellen's line about Catherine Deneuve was more than

a joke, and Fanny knew it. Madonna or Julia Roberts would have been better choices, in Fanny's opinion, but Catherine Deneuve was Henry's favorite actress, and by mentioning her, Fanny sensed that her mother was telling her father that everything would be all right. It was a signal. Fanny wasn't sure why, but sometimes this way of communicating seemed more direct than actually saying what was on one's mind, and easier.

"Thank you," Henry said, exchanging a look with Ellen. And Fanny's perception was confirmed.

The fact that Henry had brought two bags of Whoppers and french fries home from Burger King was another sign, an unspoken apology.

Henry had never liked fast-food restaurants, never took Fanny to Hardee's or McDonald's or Burger King on Saturdays or after school for a special treat.

"Mr. Dibble goes," Fanny would say. "And so does Mom. Even though I know she doesn't like the food."

"I'm not Mr. Dibble. And I'm not your mother. I'm your father. And just thinking of eating that food churns my stomach and sets my teeth on edge." Trying to lighten the mood, he'd often add, "I'd rather eat wind sauce and air pudding."

Henry took her other places, of course, places Fanny enjoyed—small, dark taverns near State Street that served thick, rare hamburgers like the kind Henry made at home, or the Union Terrace behind the Memorial Union building on campus. They'd always get cheese sandwiches at the deli counter in the Union, and eat them outside if the weather was nice. At the Union Terrace, round metal tables and chairs painted in bright colors—yellow, green, orange—were scattered here and there near the shore of Lake Mendota like handfuls of M&Ms. Fanny always searched for an orange table, and she always situated her chair so that she would face the water. This way she could watch the sailboats skim across the lake. She could watch birds ride the wind, then swoop down to peck about at the water's foamy edge. And she could watch the students. Students with pierced lips and noses. Students stooped from backpacks crammed with too many books. Students zipping by on Rollerblades, leaving musky trails behind them. Students folded together, their faces concealed, kissing. They all seemed so exotic to her.

Occasionally, they'd run into some of Henry's graduate students, and they'd share their table with them. The students would bring pitchers of beer and bags of popcorn. Although Fanny was shy around them, she'd lean into the table and listen to them talk about painting as if nothing else in the world mattered. *She* wasn't terribly interested in painting; she was observing. Observing how one student twisted strands of her hair and looked sidewise at anyone who walked by. Observing how another chewed on his paper cup until the rim was tattered and flakes of wax had piled up on the table in front of him.

Observing how yet another spoke with her hands flapping rapidly so that Fanny didn't know if she should look at her face or her fingers.

Fanny would pretend her lemonade was beer, licking her lips after every slow sip. Often she'd create stories about the students in her head—who was dating whom; who secretly had a crush on whom; who was so afraid of Henry she'd turn around and retreat if she saw him coming toward her in the hallway.

On their way home from these outings, Henry would invariably say something like, "Now, wasn't that better than McDonald's? One-of-a-kind places have much more character."

And even if Fanny had had the most wonderful time, she would only go so far as to say something like, "It was fun," because in her mind the issue wasn't the merits of McDonald's, but the power of Henry's will.

However, one Sunday last spring, on the road, driving home from a weekend of shopping and museum-going in Chicago, there had been nothing like the Union Terrace, no homey taverns to be found.

"I'm *so* hungry," Fanny had said repeatedly. Eyeing a sign for a Burger King, she asked to stop. "Please," she said. "Burger King is my favorite."

"I'll find someplace better," said Henry. "You know I won't eat at a place like that. Awful," he said, shaking his head. "Worse than awful. I'd rather eat—"

"—wind sauce and air pudding," Fanny cut in. "I know, I know." She rolled her eyes. "Dumb. Not funny," she whispered.

They passed the Burger King. And a McDonald's and a Wendy's and eventually another Burger King. Fanny watched each one whiz by, just a blur through the car window that passed out of sight completely in a matter of seconds.

Fanny was becoming more and more irritable. Her stomach growled and her head ached. Incessantly, she rolled the car window up and down, up and down, hoping that it would annoy Henry.

Miles and miles of attempting to annoy Henry.

Henry tried in his own way, taking a couple of exits that seemed promising. He found a diner that looked perfect from a distance, only to discover that it was closed on Sundays.

"Oh, well," said Henry, "we're not far from Madison now. We can just eat at home. I'll make something special."

"I'd rather eat wind sauce and air pudding," said Fanny, staring at the back of her father's head with narrow, narrow eyes.

Ellen, who had been napping most of the way, raised her head and muttered in a groggy voice, "Sometimes you two are so alike it's frightening." Then she settled down again, slumped against the locked door. She hadn't even bothered to open her eyes.

❄   ❄   ❄

Fanny could call to mind that day as if it had been yesterday. And obviously Henry remembered it, too. *"I remember more than you think."* Perhaps he could even recollect Stupid Hunts and Marie, and maybe she'd ask him about them sometime. After all, he had mentioned milk with a red licorice straw. Fanny always assumed that her father had difficulty drawing back memories of her childhood, as if they were hidden in deep, murky water and required something beyond ordinary human abilities to bring them to the surface.

Henry laughed again, and everything about him that could be imposing fell away. "Catherine Deneuve," he chuckled.

Watching him, Fanny wished that there was some way to slip into his skin for even a brief amount of time. Just long enough to glimpse her mother and herself from his point of view.

"Finished," said Henry, pushing his plate aside.

"We have birthday cake," Fanny said, almost as a question, glancing at her mother.

Ellen nodded. "I'll put coffee on."

"Mom and I already ate some," Fanny explained to Henry. "But it still looks nice."

"Sounds great to me," said Henry. "We need a fire," he added, rising from the table. "Let's eat in the living room."

"I'll be in charge of the cake," Fanny told them.

Dinner followed Henry out of the kitchen.

After preparing the coffeemaker, Ellen joined Fanny by the counter. Fanny was arranging candles on Henry's cake.

"Need help?" Ellen asked.

"Nah." Fanny looked up at her mother.

"Hang in there," said Ellen. "I think he's ready to explain what happened." She pecked Fanny's forehead. "I'll get a knife and forks and plates. But we don't have to wait for the coffee—that machine is so temperamental. It'll be a while."

Fanny could hear the plates rattle down the hallway. "Be right there," she called after her mother.

While the coffeemaker spit and hissed, Fanny worked on the cake. She had begun a border with the candles, but changed her mind when it was halfway completed. She pulled the candles out, smoothed the frosting with her finger. Instead, she wrote the word HOME across the cake in capital letters using all the little candles she could find. She was careful not to interfere too badly with the iced letters that said HAPPY BIRTHDAY, HENRY, or the dense, sugary roses.

Fanny peered at the cake. Something is missing, she thought.

Just prior to lighting the candles and marching out to her parents, she drew the letters D and G vertically in the frosting with her finger, combining them with the letter O from the word HOME to spell the word DOG. The words formed a cross. "Dog. Home," Fanny said out loud.

In the dark room with only the light from the fireplace and the candles, she didn't suppose anyone would notice.

7

It happened the way a sneeze happens. She could feel it creeping up. It was abrupt and swift and involuntary. There were little explosions going off all over inside her. If she hadn't had skin holding everything together, she was certain parts of her would have ended up on the ceiling and under the bookshelf. It happened in a flash, and when it was over, she had fallen completely in love with Dinner.

How could she not?

Dinner stayed beside Fanny throughout the course of

the evening, pushing her chin onto Fanny's thigh and keeping it there for long periods of time. Her tail wagged; her eyebrows danced. Dinner's soft, thick, brindled coat was mostly a creamy tan color with patches of black and brown across her back and on her tail and sides. The hair on her paws was white. Fanny held her hand so that it resembled one of her mother's gardening tools, her fingers rigid and spread out, and raked patterns into the tufts near Dinner's neck—swirls, hearts, figure eights. Fanny didn't seem to notice Dinner's unpleasant breath, or mind that whenever she bent down to kiss Dinner on her head, Dinner reached upward quickly and licked Fanny's face.

It couldn't have been a better scenario if Fanny had written and directed it herself. The living room was shadowed and toasty. Light from the fire flickered on the walls and every place Fanny looked. The walls seemed to converge, drawing in toward the fireplace, the room filled only with good things, the right words. For minutes at a time Fanny felt removed from it all, as though she were watching it from afar and envying the girl she saw sitting with the dog.

When they had finished their cake, the coffee cups were empty, Henry's birthday gifts had been opened, and the wrapping paper had been balled and flipped into the fire, Henry told the story of Dinner.

❄   ❄   ❄

"I had known about her for a few weeks," Henry began. "Diane, the secretary at the art office, told me about her. She belonged to a friend of hers who had recently gone through a divorce. The woman needed to move to a small apartment. She couldn't keep the dog, couldn't afford her anymore."

"What about the husband?" Fanny asked.

"According to Diane, he's already living in California. Out of the picture," said Henry. "At first, Diane wanted Dinner herself, but she couldn't persuade her husband to agree to having another pet. Diane was the one who told me what a sweet disposition the dog had; that she was three years old; that she was part German shepherd, part yellow Lab; that she was well trained, easy to be around. 'The perfect dog,' Diane said."

Henry paused to shift and readjust himself. He was sitting on the floor with Ellen, their backs against the couch, their hands clasped, their arms woven together.

Fanny took note that her mother was wearing the brooch from her father.

"Hard floor, eh?" Ellen said, smiling.

"Like a pillow," said Henry.

"Do you want to move?" Ellen asked.

"No, no," said Henry. "This is kind of nice. Let's stay put."

They cuddled.

"Let's get back to Dinner," Fanny said eagerly.

"Yesterday," Henry continued, "when I went to the

art office to call you"—Henry tipped his head to Ellen, his eyes fleetingly sad—"to say that I wouldn't be coming to the party, I saw a photo of Dinner on the staff bulletin board. The photo was taped to a notice listing all the vital information concerning her adoption. I'm not sure why, but everything seemed wrong to me—turning sixty, the party, my career—everything but the dog in that damned photo. *She* seemed right. So, on impulse, I called the number to say that I was interested. I went to see her, played with her for a bit, said I'd take her—and did. I think the woman was glad I knew Diane; I think she saw that as a nice connection." Henry nodded. "I'd never thought about getting an older dog before. Dinner and I got to know each other at the cabin. She's a champ with a tennis ball. Unbelievably tireless."

Henry went on. "My perspective was all shaken up . . . and there was something so simple and common and striking about that dog. . . . something about the whole thing that, like I said—just seemed right."

"So you already had Dinner with you when you stopped home with the balloons?" Fanny inquired.

"Yes."

"But what would you have done if we were home?"

Henry cleared his throat. "Actually, I saw you drive away. I had been waiting around the corner, sitting in the car, feeling bad, hoping you'd leave. If you hadn't, I suppose I would have put the note and balloons on the porch . . . and sneaked off? I don't know."

The stack of logs in the fireplace collapsed suddenly, emphasizing Henry's words and startling Fanny. Sparks flew up.

"What about her name?" Fanny asked. "Do you know where it comes from?"

"I wondered about that, too," Henry replied. "The owner simply said that she and her husband couldn't decide on a name for the longest time. Eventually, they realized that the dog only came when they called her for dinner. Hence, her name." Henry grinned and shrugged. "Dinner."

Each time Dinner's name was spoken, her eyes jumped with alertness and her ears lifted. Fanny and her parents laughed.

"What a good girl you are," Fanny told Dinner, petting her. "You are so beautiful. A princess."

The fire was dying. Henry crept over to the fireplace to poke at the smoldering remains and put a new log on. He nudged Fanny's toes with his elbow.

With a tightened jaw, Fanny asked the question that had begun to nag at her. "Was the woman sad?" It sounded funny to call her "the woman," but Fanny didn't know her name; she didn't want to know. She was glad that her father hadn't mentioned it.

"Yes," Henry said calmly. "Very. But don't worry. She was genuinely relieved to find a new home for Dinner. And don't worry about me, either. This will work."

"Does she have any kids?"

"She has a son about your age. But she said that neither he nor his father was very attached to Dinner."

That was difficult for Fanny to believe, but nonetheless her father's comment put her at ease.

When Henry was settled again, he talked in great detail about Dinner's retrieving ability. "I've never seen anything like it. I threw the tennis ball as high as I could, and she'd catch it nearly every time." The manner in which Henry spoke was round and bright, and if his words could be seen as well as heard, Fanny thought that they would be oranges, tumbling from his mouth and rolling across the floor in loops. "The best was when I'd lob the ball high and far, and she'd race to catch it on the first bounce. Her legs would lift off the ground, and she'd lunge for the ball with incredible grace. I could see the muscles rippling through her body. It was absolutely amazing to watch."

They talked—mostly about Dinner—and sat quietly until the fire had died down again and Ellen said, "I'm exhausted." She yawned and rose.

"Likewise," said Henry.

"Are you going to bed?" Fanny asked.

"*I* am," Ellen answered dully, her eyes half-closed. She headed for the staircase.

Henry nodded and rose too, first on one knee, then up slowly with a creak.

Fanny felt strange—a combination of excitement and fatigue, but then it had been an unusual day. *Two* days.

Two days in which time seemed to have been measured in a haphazard fashion; two days in which unreal and unpredictable things had become common. She swallowed a yawn. "May Dinner sleep in my room?" Fanny asked her father.

"If she wants to," Henry replied. "At the cabin she wandered throughout the night and ended up sleeping by the front door."

While Henry locked the doors, Fanny gathered some of Dinner's things to take up to her room—a rawhide bone, a rubber snowman, a dilapidated dove-colored afghan with holes as big as quarters—and waited at the foot of the stairs. She could hear Dinner in the kitchen, and she'd forgotten how she loved the sound of a dog drinking: *lap, lap, lap, lap, lup, lup, lup, lup, lip, lip, lip, lip* . . .

Dinner and Henry joined Fanny, and together they ascended the stairs.

Ellen, who was coming out of the bathroom, nearly collided with Fanny. "Night, Fan," she said.

"Night, Mom."

"We made it," Ellen whispered into Fanny's ear. Then she kissed it tenderly.

Henry walked Fanny to her door. "Good night, Dinner," he said. "And good night, Miss Fancy, my sweet one-of-a-kind snowflake."

"Night, Dad." Fanny wanted to add, "I'm glad you're

home," but she didn't. And she thought that Henry wanted to say something else, too.

He winked at her and vanished down the hallway.

While Dinner sniffed around the bedroom, Fanny prepared a space for her between the dresser and the radiator, folding Dinner's afghan into a rectangle as best she could, given the afghan's shabby state. "There," she said, patting the afghan. "This is your bed."

Dinner slunk over to Fanny, turned a circle, then dropped heavily with a sigh. She became compact as a suitcase, with her legs pulled in, her tail tucked under her legs, and her head curled snugly against her chest. She batted her eyes and sighed again.

"Please, sleep here," Fanny said. "This is your room, too, you know." She was on her knees peering directly into Dinner's eyes. It was difficult for Fanny to turn her gaze away.

But that's exactly what she managed to do. She was tired. Her own familiar bed had never looked so soft and thick and good. Fanny switched her fan on, and she left the door ajar in case Dinner wanted to leave. As she wrapped her puffy comforter around her and jiggled her legs to warm the sheets, she concentrated intensely and said the word *stay* in her head.

STAY.

They both fell asleep in minutes. The sheets were still icy.

Fanny awoke in the middle of the night. She heard Dinner's tags rattle and her nails click against the floor. The sounds had been part of a dream, sounds that grew more clear until Fanny could almost feel them, and she started. She was crestfallen when she realized what the sounds truly were, when she realized that Dinner had risen and left the bedroom.

However, when Fanny woke up in the morning, she was elated to find Dinner back in her room, lying smack in the middle of the afghan. As soon as Fanny stirred, Dinner stretched and hurried to the side of the bed, her tail wagging fiercely. They greeted each other with pats (from Fanny) and licks (from Dinner), and they inadvertently did a funny little dance as Fanny, with Dinner at her heels, stumbled putting on her socks and robe.

They bumped into the door, and Fanny's Advent calendar fell to the floor. She picked it up and refastened it. Because of the confusion of the past two days, Fanny had forgotten all about it.

Ellen had bought the Advent calendar for Fanny when she was a toddler. Fanny took it out of her file cabinet every year and hung it in her room. Instead of windows or doors, there were numbered tabs on the calendar, which, when pulled, revealed chubby angels with sturdy wings and red mittens carrying lanterns. The angels were hidden behind snow-laden pine trees. The angel for the twenty-fourth day was taller than the rest, and slender. More solemn looking, even rueful. She carried one large lighted candle; her head was wreathed in stars. Against the midnight blue sky, she glowed. Fanny had named her Sparkle right from the start.

Fanny tried to remember exactly what Sparkle looked like each year. But she always made herself wait until Christmas Eve to see how closely the picture in her mind matched the real thing. It was a point of pride with her—to wait.

With Dinner at her side, Fanny slid back the tabs she had already pulled, concealing the angels that had reappeared this year. She closed her eyes and counted to ten. Then she said, "Watch this, Dinner." Fanny tugged each and every tab as quickly as she could, drawing out all the angels. Even Sparkle. She was as beautiful as ever.

"Now let's go wake up the house," Fanny said to Dinner.

It may not have been December twenty-fifth yet, but as far as Fanny was concerned, Christmas had arrived.

8

It was December twenty-third.

Then it was December twenty-fourth.

And then it was December twenty-fifth.

And Dinner managed to accomplish what neither Ellen nor Henry ever had; Dinner provided for Fanny a sense of calm concerning Christmas. Because Dinner was there—and belonged to Fanny—nothing else seemed so important or crucial. Dinner eased Fanny's expectations. Any other year, Fanny would have been disappointed.

She would have protested—at least with a sigh or momentary sullenness—even the smallest changes or imperfections. But not this year. Not since Dinner had arrived. Who cared if they hadn't baked all the different kinds of cookies? Who cared if Ellen forgot to buy red gumdrops to use as the garnish for the glazed ham and had to settle for cranberries? Who cared if Henry fell asleep during his traditional Christmas Eve reading of "The Snow Queen" and Fanny had to finish it herself? Dinner eclipsed it all. The days passed just as they should have, like the turning of pages in a quietly lovely book.

Fanny's newly acquired attitude faltered only once, and briefly. That was when Henry received his Christmas gift from her. She was always slightly apprehensive when this part of the morning came upon them, because she wanted to please him, and he was difficult to please.

Without hesitation, Henry said that he was delighted by her gift, and she could tell that he was being truthful. "I'll use these," he told her. "I will definitely use these." He lowered his head, his eyes veiled, and carefully studied the contents of the cardboard box he had just slit open with his Swiss army knife. The box held about a dozen vases, bottles, and bowls that Fanny had found in the antique stores and resale shops near campus. Henry plucked his reading glasses from the pocket of his sport jacket and hooked the wire bows over his ears. The glasses were perched at the very tip of his nose, and he went back and forth from looking through them to looking over them. The lenses glinted. Henry rubbed the lip of one vase and raised another vase up to the light. "Perhaps these will get my painting moving again."

"Good," Fanny said in a hushed voice, squeezing her shoulders in and up toward her ears. She smiled with relief. In no time at all, her heart slowed down and she was back to her old new-self.

It had been months since Henry had finished a painting, although he would sit in his studio for hours on end, every chance he could get. Fanny thought that her father's artwork revealed his personality better than even a photograph of him did. He painted in oil on canvas and panel. His paintings were carefully rendered arrangements of bottles, cups, saucers, vases, and bowls. The well-ordered groupings of vessels usually sat on highly polished tabletops. Sometimes he would add a Moonglow pear or a Golden Russet apple balancing on the edge of the table. Sometimes he would place something discordant, like a rusty knife, in an exquisite, clear handblown vase, or paint a vase that had just been broken. Sometimes there would be a sere, saffron landscape behind the table. But more often than not, it was the vessels alone, against a simple background. The vessels were usually opaque, and the perspective from which they were painted was such that one couldn't see the insides of them.

Once Fanny had said to her father, "I always imagine

the bowls and jars filled with wonderful things. Like chocolate and peppermints and bubble bath."

"Huh," Henry had mumbled in response, sizing up the painting on his easel. "I always thought of them as being empty. Barren. Remote. I assumed that that's what everyone thought."

Regardless of her interpretation of his work, she never ceased to marvel at it. How can paint from a tube and mere brushes re-create water droplets on a pear or the pinprick of light on the handle of a teacup? Somehow what Henry painted was more real to Fanny than the actual objects.

While Fanny and Ellen opened their presents, Henry returned to his box from Fanny. From time to time, he stared off, vacantly. Fanny knew that he was thinking about painting. She recognized the look.

She saw the look again, later in the day, when they were ice skating on the green across the street. By now, Fanny was overfed and somewhat sleepy. She was wearing three of her gifts—a bulky wool sweater patterned with an intricate design of cables and ribs, mittens that Ellen had knitted, and a mother-of-pearl bracelet that looked like a ring of iridescent seeds.

When they had first come out, Henry and Fanny passed a hockey puck back and forth while Ellen skated backward, limning the edge of the rink. Dinner bounded joyfully from one side of the small park to the other, seemingly excited by the cold air and the few slow, lingering snowflakes. She snapped at the snowflakes. She chased the puck. She sniffed the tree trunks. Her legs twisted, and she lost her balance on the ice just like Fanny remembered Bambi doing in the Disney movie.

This was only the second time that Fanny had been skating this year. Her skates still felt a bit foreign. Last year when Fanny had needed new skates, Henry had insisted that she get her first pair of hockey skates. "You'll like them better than figure skates," he had told her. "I'll get you a hockey stick to go with them, and then we can play together. I'll teach you a thing or two."

At first, Fanny had missed her figure skates. She missed the row of jagged points on the front of the blades that allowed her to stop. Stopping with hockey skates was difficult, but she was learning. Henry could do it expertly. He'd bring his skates together and turn them to the side with a sharp, quick motion that would send up a spray of ice and make a cold, clean *shishhh*. Hockey skates also looked boxy and thick compared to her figure skates. To alleviate this, Fanny had dotted and striped the toes with red nail polish and changed the laces from white to magenta. She had to admit that by the end of last winter she had grown fond of the skates. Her feet had finally felt comfortable in them. However, now that it was a new season, she had to start that process all over again.

Thwack! Fanny slapped the puck to Henry as hard as

she could. It sailed between his feet and landed in a snowbank. He didn't even notice.

"Daydreaming?" she yelled.

No answer.

Fanny skated over to her father. Her steamy breath curled around her neck and dissipated. "You missed the puck," she told him.

"What? Oh," Henry said indistinctly.

Fanny stared at her father staring away. That's when she realized that he was thinking about painting again. A snowflake caught in his eyebrow.

"I guess I've had enough," he finally said. "My wrists are sore and my knees aren't up to it. I'm going to call it quits with hockey for today. Let's just skate." Henry laid his hockey stick down and floated away slowly across the ice.

Of course, by this hour it was dark, and the street lamp in the far corner of the park was on. It seemed to Fanny that night not only came early, but quickly, as if the sun were tied to a string and suddenly yanked away. Fanny tossed her hockey stick into the shadows near her father's and scurried off after him.

Rarf. Rarf-rarf-rarf. Dinner pranced up behind Fanny. She crossed in front of Fanny, then circled her wide.

"Here, Dinner," Fanny said, smacking her thighs. "Come."

Dinner came.

"Sit," Fanny added firmly.

Dinner sat.

Fanny unhooked Dinner's leash from around her own waist and put it back on the dog. "Pull me," Fanny commanded. But Dinner didn't understand. She wanted only to face Fanny and jump, to be petted, to be stroked behind her ears, to lick Fanny's cheeks, to fetch the tennis ball in Fanny's coat pocket, to play her own way. "Okay, then let's skate together," said Fanny as though she were talking to her best friend, working out a compromise. "Let's chase Dad."

They found a rhythm. Dinner led the way and Fanny skated briskly to keep up. She would glide, glide, then let herself be pulled for a few seconds. It was exactly what she had wanted in the first place. Fanny watched their shadows grow and shrink and grow again. When her shadow was dramatically elongated and pointy, Fanny waved her arms and hands wildly. I'm a carrot monster, she thought. Better yet, an icicle monster. Then, with her fingers crossed inside her mittens for good luck, Fanny tried to reverse and move backward, but she got tangled in Dinner's leash and fell. So Henry caught up with them before they caught up with him.

The three of them joined Ellen.

"My mother," Fanny said in the faintest whisper, her mittened hand at her mouth, while Ellen formed a figure eight.

Ellen moved fluently, sliding from one foot to the other, her hands running downward along her legs, then reaching out, her gloved fingers curling and uncurling. When she turned her head toward Fanny and Henry to smile, she wobbled. She finished and took a bow.

Henry clapped.

"You're good," said Fanny.

"Not really. But thank you."

"Better than me."

"What I am is cold," said Ellen.

"Home?" said Henry.

"Home," said Ellen, nodding.

"How about one lap together first?" asked Fanny.

Off they went. Henry hummed a carol. Fanny moved her head up and around and over and down.

Ellen grinned. "What are you doing?" she asked.

"Making a figure eight," Fanny replied, blushing. "Imagining it."

Ellen took Fanny's elbow and coaxed her into a little dance. "When I was a girl," said Ellen, "Grandpa John told me that it wasn't figure eights I was forming, but rather the symbol for infinity."

"The symbol for infinity is the same as an eight?" Fanny asked.

"Not exactly," Ellen replied. "It's lying down. This way." Ellen drew it with her finger. "Horizontal."

"In-fin-i-ty." Fanny pronounced it slowly. "That's the word Kai had to spell with the pieces of ice in 'The Snow Queen.' "

"No," said Henry. "That's eternity."

Fanny wrinkled her nose. "Oh," she said. "Don't they mean the same thing?"

"They're similar," Henry answered, "but they're definitely different."

Eternity. Infinity. Fanny made a mental note to look them up in the dictionary at home.

A wooden stake sprayed with a runny splotch of fluorescent orange paint marked the halfway point. When they reached it, Henry announced suddenly, "Race to the bench! Last one has to bring in some firewood! Go!"

Fanny took off, her skates clicking and clacking against the ice. She sped ahead with reckless abandon. Out of the corner of her eye, she could see everyone: her father, her mother, her dog. And everything became so alive and heightened and dazzling. Everything stunned and pleased her: The way her father's voice had boomed in the night and still rang in her ears. The way the wind pulled a strand of her mother's hair across her face, dividing it perfectly in half. The way Dinner's tongue hung out of her mouth like a pink sock. The way the air she breathed through her nose felt icy as it entered her, then burned inside her head. The way the street lamp turned into a halo when she squinted at it. The way the matted pellets of snow on her new mittens became diamonds. The way her toes were so cold they were hot. The way the big, lone, skeletal elm tree in the distance looked like a giant wineglass.

How could one moment be crammed with so much?

Fanny could barely contain herself. "I love you," she called gleefully, not thinking of one person or one thing or anything specific.

"Me, too," said Henry.

"Me, three," said Ellen.

Dinner barked and won the race.

On Christmas night, Fanny dreamed.

She was waiting at the dining room table. "What's for dinner?" she asked.

"Wind sauce and air pudding!" Henry bellowed.

"I'd rather skate," said Ellen.

It was snowing inside the house. Flakes as big as milkweed fluff fell gently. Through the whiteness, Dinner emerged. She was standing up on her hind legs, humanlike, carrying a tray. As she came closer, Fanny noticed that she was skating and that the tray held three glasses of milk, each with a red licorice straw. The floor had turned to ice.

Although they were in the dining room, Fanny saw that there were brilliant orange embers in the fireplace and that all four burners of the stove were turned on. Four flaming blue crowns.

"Elm trees without their leaves look like wineglasses," said Henry.

"Don't lick the snow off the porch railing," said Ellen. "Your tongue will stick."

And then Fanny was standing by the front window, rubbing the steam away with her hand. "I'm waiting for someone," she said.

"Mary?" said Ellen.

"Nellie?" said Henry. "A boy?"

"The Snow Queen," said Fanny.

"Why do you like her so?" asked Ellen. "She's evil."

"I like her, too," said Henry.

A shadow passed over the house. Dinner came running. And Fanny woke up.

9

❄

With Mary Dibble in Florida, Fanny spent the bulk
of her time with Dinner. For the most part, they were
inseparable. Fanny did, however, sleep at Jessie Bayer's
house one night, along with three other girls; and she
went sledding the following morning with a passel of
classmates. Although Fanny enjoyed herself—especially
at the slumber party, where they stayed awake long past
midnight, gobbling fudge and watching a videotape of
Sixteen Candles (which Fanny had already seen seven
times)—she missed Dinner. When Fanny returned, Din-

ner met her with a grand outpouring of affection complete with her rapid-fire tail and a wiggle fit. If Fanny had had a tail of her own, it would have been waggling just as vigorously.

"What am I going to do when winter break is over?" Fanny asked Dinner. "What am I going to do when school starts again in January?"

At least once a day, and usually twice, Fanny walked Dinner on the railroad tracks that ran parallel to her street, one block away. Because you could see into the backyards on either side of the tracks, Fanny turned her head from side to side, looking, feeling somewhat intrusive. As a little girl, she had wished that the big, slow train chugged through her own backyard and was jealous of the neighborhood kids who were lucky enough to live in these choice houses. After about an eighth of a mile, the houses on the north side of the tracks ended; a scruffy field took their place. At this point, a tangle of trails began. The main trail, narrow and twisty, wound through the field and then through thick brush and old oak trees. It jumped a creek, bordered a cemetery, and eventually looped back to the tracks, forming a lopsided circle segmented by trails even more narrow and twisty than the main one.

The tracks and the trails and the woods were the closest thing to heaven for a dog that Fanny could think of. Dinner seemed supremely happy here. Fanny always let her off her leash to run with other dogs and to chase squirrels. On any given walk, Fanny and Dinner came across several of both—dogs and squirrels.

During the brief period in which she had owned Nellie, Fanny had brought her to the tracks and trails, but only three or four times. Nellie was overcome with fear at the sight of other dogs—big ones, playful ones—and she would make herself half her size and press herself to the ground, unwilling to go on.

Now, on her outings with Dinner, Fanny couldn't help but think of Nellie, and she wondered if Dinner would have frightened her with her bulk and exuberance. While they walked, Fanny told Dinner about Nellie. "She's kind of like a sister to you," Fanny explained. "Nellie is. But I don't know if you'll ever meet her." Fanny frowned at her boots. "She was still a puppy when she left."

Dinner's angular face tilted, as if to listen more carefully.

"Let's see," said Fanny, thinking, "what else should I tell you?" She jerked the collar of her coat up around her neck and breathed down inside the slight, furry wall it formed. "I probably should start with Dad . . ."

On and on they meandered, and on and on Fanny talked. Fanny told Dinner all the things she needed to know, things Fanny needed to say. She realized as it was happening how good it felt to express certain thoughts in this manner. "He's impossible sometimes. And unpredictable. Especially if his painting isn't going well or if he's blocked. *He* made Nellie leave, you know. It was his fault."

Dinner's tail thumped against Fanny's leg.

"I see," said Fanny. She tried to lighten her tone. "I'm glad you understand. So always be on your best behavior. Then you won't have anything to worry about."

It was early Thursday afternoon, their second walk of the day. The snow on the paths was dirty and trampled, but the snow in the distance that was caked to the tree trunks and the snow that enveloped the hill sloping up toward the railroad tracks looked untouched and pure. It sparkled in the sunlight.

There was a circular clearing nearby where Fanny played fetch with Dinner. As they approached it, Fanny dug into her pocket for Dinner's tennis ball. Dinner sensed something at once. Something good. Then she pranced about, knowing for certain what came next. Fanny threw the ball and Dinner darted after it. One, two, three times Fanny threw the ball. One, two, three times Dinner retrieved it.

Brown, brittle oak leaves poked up through the snow. Fanny made believe that the clearing was a gigantic oak-leaf pie with a crunchy sugar-snow crust. Dinner's paw prints crisscrossed the open area like the slits Ellen made in her pie crusts to let the steam escape while baking.

After each retrieval, Dinner dropped the ball at Fanny's feet. It didn't take long for the ball to become soggy and filthy, but Fanny wasn't put off by it. If Fanny waited an extra few seconds to unwrap a peppermint and pop it into her mouth, or to brush her hair out of her eyes, or to pick a leaf off the ball before throwing it again, Dinner barked.

"My, you're impatient."

She barked once more.

"My best friend?" said Fanny. "How nice of you to ask. Her name is Mary."

Rarf.

"Yes, you'll get to meet her."

Dinner could barely sit still. She lurched forward spasmodically, anticipating the ball. Little tremors shot from her tail to her nose. *Rarf-arf-arf.*

Finally, Fanny set her arm in position and tossed the ball. But she kept talking. "We're kind of like sisters, too," she said, thinking of her telephone conversation with Mary from Florida. "Mary and me. You and Nellie."

Dinner came back and let the ball fall from her mouth. She was panting so hard her breath came out in bursts that shrouded her face. The hair on her chin and a few of her whiskers were lacy with frost. Instead of barking, Dinner stretched. A single soft groan came from her throat.

"What do I like?" said Fanny, stretching, too. "Oh, thin pizza with just pepperoni . . . and fake snow in old black-and-white movies . . . and making sparks in my hair by pulling my shirt off in the dark really fast."

Dinner placed her paw on the ball and pulled back. The ball spun.

Fanny laughed. "Okay, I know you want to play. End of conversation."

Fanny threw the tennis ball a total of fifteen times. Fifteen was her lucky number. She had been born on March fifteenth.

"That's it," Fanny announced. "We're done." She put the ball into a plastic bag and stuffed it back inside her pocket. It was becoming routine for Fanny to give Dinner a dog biscuit at this point in their walk, and so she did. Dinner ate it quickly, then licked her snout.

A squirrel skittered by, its tail swaying evenly, brushing wings into the snow. Dinner saw it and was tempted by it, but Fanny clicked her tongue and sternly commanded, "Stay!" She was testing Dinner.

Clearly, Dinner wanted to chase the squirrel—her eyes flicked between the squirrel and Fanny—but she stayed. This gave Fanny great satisfaction. "Good girl!" Fanny said sweetly. She patted Dinner's side, making a hollow sound. "Come on," said Fanny. And Dinner followed her like her shadow.

On their way back to the railroad tracks, Fanny spotted the red cap for the third time since Christmas. "There he is again," she said in a tight whisper. It was a boy wearing the red cap, a boy about her age. He had never come close enough for Fanny to tell his age for certain. He had never come close enough for Fanny to know the color of his eyes or hair. All she knew was the red cap.

It appeared among some tall bushes like a rare bird. In the time it took Fanny to glance at Dinner and look back, the cap was gone. This had been the case the other times Fanny had seen the boy. All of a sudden, the cap had been visible between distant trees or at the exact point where the trail curved behind a hill. And then— *blink*—it had disappeared.

Fanny met many people in the trails, but they all seemed to have a purpose for being there. They either had dogs with them or were walking briskly, obviously for exercise, their arms swinging, backs straight. The boy's purpose was unclear.

The boy didn't frighten Fanny, but having noticed him three times in a span of only five days left her feeling both uneasy and curious. She wondered if he was watching her.

Fanny had to fight an urge to chase after the boy as she led Dinner in the opposite direction, the direction of home. They angled through the field, walked the tracks, and cut across the green. Fanny was jogging up the sidewalk in front of her house when a terrible thought occurred to her: The boy in the red cap is the son of the woman who owned Dinner. He wants her back.

She stumbled and fell, scraping her knee on the cement, tearing her favorite jeans.

❄ ❄ ❄

New Year's Eve. Fanny whiled the evening away half-heartedly doing schoolwork, aimlessly flipping through the channels on TV, and making trips to the dining room to snack on the elegant hors d'oeuvres that had taken her mother all afternoon to prepare. Fanny had said no to going to a party at a friend's house, choosing to stay home because of the boy in the red cap. She couldn't rid her mind of the thought that he was surely spying on her with the intention of trying somehow to take Dinner back. And how could she have fun at a party if she were worrying so?

It was when her sense of dread dwindled that she would make her trips to the dining room. "I'm being silly," she said to Dinner repeatedly. "I know I'm being silly."

"*Who's* silly?" asked Stuart Walker.

"Oh," said Fanny shyly, "I was just talking to the dog."

It had become customary over the past few years for Stuart and Adele Walker to spend New Year's Eve at the Swanns'. Instead of dinner, Ellen and Henry served hors d'oeuvres and champagne. That was all. But there was more food than if Ellen had cooked a five-course meal.

Stuart and Adele were, Fanny guessed, her parents' closest friends. The Walkers were both in their sixties, their children grown. Stuart taught photography at the university; Adele was a nurse. More than any other couple

Fanny knew, the Walkers looked like each other. They both wore glasses and had short hair the color of French vanilla ice cream that they parted on the left. When they stood shoulder to shoulder, everything matched up— elbows, waists, knees, chins.

"Your mother's outdone herself again," said Stuart, patting his belly.

"Yeah."

The top of the dining room table looked to Fanny like a Lilliputian town seen from above and afar. A small mountain of pâté surrounded by juniper sprigs and kum- quats was the focal point. Trays and chafing dishes of stuffed mushrooms, meatballs, crab puffs, oysters wrapped in bacon, and canapés of all sorts and kinds stretched like hills and valleys from one end of the table to the other. Some of the food sat on large puckered lettuce leaves; the trays and dishes sat on a sea blue tablecloth.

"These are the best," Stuart said, holding up one of the bacon-wrapped oysters by its toothpick and twirling it with a flourish.

"Yuck," said Fanny, wrinkling her nose. She thought that oysters looked unappealing and tasted worse.

"Good," said Stuart, reaching for another. "All the more for me. By the way, do you know what these are called?" he asked.

Fanny shook her head.

"Angels on horseback," Stuart replied.

"Really?" Fanny flashed Stuart a disbelieving smirk.

"Really, truly. Angels on horseback. Great name, don't you think?"

Fanny eyed the platter of brown, curly *things* stabbed with toothpicks. "It doesn't really fit, though." The name conjured up a drastically different image in her mind. The name made her think of sweet and delicate pastries dusted with powdered sugar. "I think they should be called slimy little globs."

Stuart laughed. He selected one of the toothpicks from the heap that had collected on his plate and stuck it in the corner of his mouth. It bounced as he spoke. "Don't mind me. Just filling my plate for the fifth time," he said in a comical voice. As he worked his way up the table, his voice became lower, more serious. "I never see you around anymore. I remember when you used to hang out at your father's studio on campus."

Fanny used to walk there occasionally after school to do her homework until he was ready to leave—although, because he'd let her draw and paint, she didn't get much work done. "That was a long time ago," she said, rotating her empty plate in her hands. "He paints mostly at home now anyway." Her upper lip disappeared under her lower one.

"I'm still fond of that photograph I took of you there," said Stuart, "fast asleep on the floor amid that overwhelming sweep of pots and things he has."

122

The photograph was black-and-white, printed in velvety tones. It hung in a simple wooden frame in Henry and Ellen's bedroom. One entire wall was devoted to it. Fanny wasn't even noticeable at first glance, almost hidden as she was among the stacks of pottery. Only a few of her stockinged toes, darkened with charcoal, were visible, poking out near the bottom of the photograph, and just a sliver of her face showed from behind a large egg-shaped pot. But, nonetheless, it was unmistakably Fanny.

"Yeah, I really had a ball there," Fanny said wistfully.

Upon hearing the word ball, Dinner raised her head smartly and quickly and snapped it around.

"Oops," said Fanny. "She knows what B-A-L-L means."

"Clever dog," said Stuart. "And some Christmas present. Your father told us all about her."

Not only to be polite, but because she thought he was a nice man and she liked him and she needed to ask him a question privately, Fanny said, "Do you want to play fetch with Dinner and me in the backyard?"

"I'd love to," Stuart answered.

They bundled up and went outside.

Under the glow of the backyard light, Fanny watched Dinner and Stuart Walker play fetch. Even though Stuart was the one throwing the ball, Dinner dropped the ball near Fanny and nosed it closer and closer to her until it touched her boot. Fanny lightly kicked the ball to Stuart.

"I guess she knows who's boss," Stuart said. "I can tell you've spent a lot of time with her." He brushed the snow off Dinner's snout and tapped her gently. "Some dog. What a good pooch you are."

"She's smart," Fanny said, nodding. She leaned toward the house, away from Stuart, and surreptitiously wiped her nose on her mitten. She had neither a handkerchief nor a tissue with her. After taking a deep breath, Fanny asked rather suddenly, "You're over sixty, aren't you?" Immediately, the words seemed indelicate to her ears and she could feel herself blush.

"Years or pounds?" Stuart replied, chuckling. He paused for the slightest moment, then said, "Yes, to both."

Fanny pressed on. "I was wondering if it's hard for you to—" Here she hesitated, almost adding, "—be that old?" She finally finished with, "—be that age?"

"Not really. But I'm guessing that you're thinking about your father, not me."

Fanny bowed her head in agreement.

"At your age, birthdays are a joy. When you're my age—your father's age—a birthday isn't necessarily something to be celebrated in that same joyous manner. It *can* be, but it can feel very strange, too. So I understand why the party was canceled. And I know about his going away for the night."

Hearing this somehow made Fanny feel better. She sighed. Her breath shot out in a steady stream like car exhaust.

Stuart continued playing with Dinner while he spoke. He didn't look at Fanny; his eyes were fixed on the tennis ball. "Knowing your father, I think this will pass."

"But . . . did anything happen when you turned sixty? Did you *do* anything?" What she really wanted to ask was: Is he all *right?* But her shyness was increasing and to be that direct seemed impossible.

"I bought a new car and I shaved my beard of twenty-some years."

"Did I know you with a beard?"

"Well, I'm sixty-seven, so I shaved it seven years ago."

"I would have been five then," Fanny said, twisting her mouth into a crooked smile, thinking. "I don't remember."

They were quiet. Then Stuart coughed—a cough that sounded forced to Fanny, as if it were intended to shake the stillness, move the conversation. It echoed in the night. And in the long silence that followed, Fanny realized that Stuart Walker was not going to reveal some crucial insight about her father or growing older. Perhaps no one could help her with this.

"Any resolutions?" Fanny asked, changing the subject completely, needing something to say.

"I'm going to reread *War and Peace*," Stuart told her. "And you?"

"Oh, I don't know. Maybe get an A in math." Fanny was lying. She already knew what her resolution would be: to keep Dinner. It would be as simple and as difficult as that.

"And my resolution," said Henry, the back door slamming, "is to start painting again—soon—or quit forever."

The words snapped like frozen twigs. Instantly filled with a panicky feeling, Fanny wondered if her father had heard her question Stuart. At the same time, she was deeply saddened by his comment.

"Don't be so hard on yourself, Henry," said Stuart. He slapped Henry on the back the way Fanny had seen her father do to many men before. Women hug, thought Fanny; men slap backs. With Henry and Stuart standing side by side, it was obvious to Fanny how much whiter Henry's hair was than Stuart's.

Henry folded his arms against his chest and shivered. "Good God, it's cold out here," he said. "What are you two doing, telling secrets?"

"No," Fanny said defensively. The cold, crisp air was causing her eyes to water.

"We were playing with Wonder Dog," said Stuart.

"Well, midnight is fast approaching," said Henry.

"Come warm up before the big event. Whoop-de-do!" There was more than a trace of sarcasm in his voice.

Once inside, they watched the replay of the famous glittery ball dropping in Times Square on TV, and they toasted the new year and one another. Henry kissed Ellen and Stuart kissed Adele and Fanny kissed Dinner.

Fanny gave Dinner two dog biscuits, and she hugged her mother for a long moment as if she would never let go.

When the Walkers soon departed, there was more hugging and back slapping and kissing and well wishing. Henry stepped out onto the porch with Stuart and Adele. Ellen began carrying trays of half-eaten food to the kitchen. Dinner lingered in the chilly hallway, sniffing at the air that rushed through the crack between the door and the doorjamb. As Fanny tried to urge Dinner back into the warm house, she heard Stuart, his voice crystalline and clear, say to Henry, "Happy New Year again, you old goat. And if you can't handle *this* dog, give me a call. I'd take her in a heartbeat."

10

❄

The Swanns' Christmas tree lay along the curbside like a discarded piece of furniture, a peculiar green chair tipped over. It was one of three trees already set out on their block. Inside the house, the ornaments and the village from beneath the tree were wrapped in musty tissue paper and boxed. The strings of lights were coiled and packed into the closet in the guest room. While Fanny and Ellen were unwinding the cottony fabric that formed the snowy hills on which the village had been sitting, Fanny found the little dog statue that her father had left for her the night he had sneaked off. She had forgotten all about it. She ran upstairs and stowed it in her file cabinet.

"I always find it uplifting to take the Christmas decorations down right away," Ellen said, her arm rising from her hip and her palm turning, dipping toward the empty-looking corner of the living room where the tree had just stood. "New Year's Day—a fresh start."

"It's kind of sad, too," Fanny offered, fiddling with a pine needle. "The end."

"What do you mean, the end? It's January first—*the* beginning."

Fanny shrugged and smiled vaguely. She sniffed her fingers; they smelled like a forest. It was the beginning, all right, the beginning of new things to worry about. Namely the boy in the red cap and Stuart Walker's comment about taking Dinner. (Fanny could do without *anyone* giving Henry ideas about how or where to get rid of her dog.) And then, of course, there was Henry's artwork to worry about. "Should we call him for lunch?" Fanny asked. Her eyes lifted in the direction of Henry's studio.

"Why don't we leave him alone? He'll come down when he's ready. With any luck, he's painting—and something's clicked."

"Will he have enough work for the show in New York?"

"Let's hope so," said Ellen. She shoved an ornament hanger under the couch with her foot. "Let's hope so."

Before Henry had gone up to his studio to paint, he had

seemed hopeful, the promise of a breakthrough shining in his eyes. He patiently brewed a pot of coffee, poured it into his red-and-black-plaid thermos bottle, hooked the most ample mug they owned on his finger, and pecked both Ellen and Fanny on the head. "It's now or never," he had said.

"No," Ellen had remarked. "Either it will work or it won't. If it doesn't today, it will soon. Right?"

Henry didn't answer. He picked up the thermos bottle with his free hand and pivoted to leave. At the door, he turned back and arched one of his wiry eyebrows.

Somehow—despite the glimmer of hope she had sensed in him—it came as little surprise to Fanny that when Henry burst into the kitchen hours later he was in a black mood. Even when she *did* anticipate one of his moods, it didn't make negotiating it any easier.

Ellen and Fanny were discussing what to make for supper when the swinging door flew open. The thermos bottle landed securely on the counter with a smack. Fanny jumped. Dinner had been curled up in the corner; she jumped, too.

"I can't paint anymore," Henry said darkly, shaking his head. "Nothing's working." The mug was still in his hand. For a second, Fanny thought he was going to throw it. He placed it solidly on the counter next to the thermos bottle with enough force to call added attention to himself, but carefully enough so as not to break it.

"Do you want me to look at what you've done so far?" Ellen asked calmly, directing her eyes to Henry, her fingers still riffling through the pages of a cookbook.

"There's nothing to look at." Henry opened and closed the cupboard he was standing beside. Open-close, open-close, open-close.

Ellen shut the cookbook. "Are you sure?"

Open-close, open-close, open-close. Henry sighed, a sigh so great that when he breathed in he seemed to be inflating like a balloon, his chest swelling, shoulders rising, the wings of his nostrils expanding. He scooped the mug off the counter, scowled at it, and walked over to the sink.

My mother is brave, Fanny thought. In situations like this, it was a struggle for Fanny to look at her father squarely. But her mother did. Fanny only managed to get as close as a wrinkle on his forehead or the top button on his shirt. She felt herself turning into a shadow. Because Fanny was looking at her mother looking at her father, she heard the noise first, then realized what it was: the clatter of Dinner's bowl and the *snap-rap-tap* of kibbles avalanching across the floor.

Henry accidentally had stepped on Dinner's metal food dish. "Damn it!" he roared.

Due to the commotion, Dinner shot up and circled the kitchen, her ears plastered back on her head.

"Henry——" said Ellen.

Fanny saw her mother hold out the dustpan to her father, but she snatched it before Henry could. "I'll do it," she said briskly.

Henry pressed his hands to his face. "I'm going for a walk," he grumbled. Kibbles crunched under his shoes. "Dog!" he said before the front door slammed.

Dinner retreated to the corner. Remaining silent, Ellen plucked another cookbook from the shelf, opened it. On her knees, Fanny cleaned up the kibbles. Some had ended up in Dinner's water dish. Already they were saturated, breaking apart—miniature fireworks exploding in a dish on the kitchen floor in a warm old house on a cold first day of the year.

The refrigerator clicked on. *Hummmmmmmm.* The hum grew louder and louder in Fanny's ears until the sound seemed to originate in her head. Like a chorus it sang: *Hummm-ummm. Himmm-immm. Him.* Him. My father. He's everywhere, she thought. She stood to turn on the transistor radio that was kept by the canisters of flour and sugar and salt.

That same afternoon, Mary Dibble came home. When the telephone rang, Fanny knew, just knew, that it was Mary.

"I've still got my jacket on," said Mary. "I called you first thing."

"May I come over?" Fanny asked.

"Meet me halfway."

"Okay. Leave in five minutes," Fanny told her. Enough time for Fanny to ask permission, brush her hair, dress for outside, get Dinner's leash and ball.

"One, two, three . . . bye!"

"Bye."

Fanny and Dinner met Mary at the corner of Willard Street and Hamilton Avenue, exactly midway between their houses. A faint smudge of light still hung above the trees. Fanny had been running in fits and starts, so she was out of breath and her cheeks were ruddy.

"Hi!" Fanny called from two houses away, waving her scarf.

When they were face-to-face, Mary gasped, "Forget hello! Whose dog?" Her eyes were the size of nickels.

"Mine."

"Yours?"

Fanny nodded slowly and smiled broadly, her teeth showing like two rows of tiny porcelain heads that were nodding and smiling, too. "Her name is Dinner."

"That's cute," said Mary. "Well? Who, what, where, when, why?"

"My dad gave her to me."

"No way. I can't believe it."

"I can barely believe it, either."

Mary bent down to pet Dinner, allowing their noses

to touch. "Cold and wet," she said, giggling. "Do you think he did it to make up for missing his party?"

"Partially, I guess. It's complicated."

"Well, who cares why? You, Fanny Swann, have got a dog," declared Mary. "The one thing you wanted most in the whole wide world."

"Ta da," said Fanny, curtsying to Dinner.

They laughed.

"Hey," said Fanny, "your face is tan. Nice."

"It's okay."

Fanny pushed her hat up to the top of her head and pulled her scarf down so that her earrings showed. She tapped one lightly with her index finger. "Remember these?"

Mary flipped her long, curly hair back behind her ears to reveal her earrings. "I've worn them every day since I opened them." Mary threw her arm around Fanny's shoulder. "I'm not used to this cold weather. I'm sort of a Floridian now. My toes are freezing off. And my fingers and my cheeks and my nose. Let's go get warm. And you have to tell me everything."

They started walking toward the Dibbles' house, matching their strides (left boot, right boot, left boot, right boot) with an attempt at a bit of fancy footwork (hop, skip, skip) like Dorothy and the Scarecrow thrown in for good measure.

❄   ❄   ❄

If the Swanns had just arrived home from a long trip, Henry wouldn't have permitted anyone to come over, even Mary. The Dibbles were different. Their house was in a constant state of amiable chaos, a steady stream of comings and goings, doors slamming, phones ringing, dogs barking, cats chattering, televisions blabbing, stereos playing, yelling, discussing, kitchen sounds, bathroom sounds, the sounds of a large family. Mary had two parents, four brothers, and one sister. Michael and Rose were in college, but they often came by for meals or to borrow something. Billy, Tom, Mary, and Joey were still at home. Whenever she was there, Fanny observed with envy that no child seemed to be the focus, and that because there was so much happening at once, if you wanted to disappear for a while you could. No one would notice.

After making hot chocolate (with vanilla and lots of miniature marshmallows), Fanny and Mary took turns recapping their lives, starting from the minute they had separated when Mary's family left for the airport. One would speak and the other would listen in rapt silence. Then there would be questions. Then they would switch roles. Meanwhile, Dinner romped in the backyard with the Dibbles' dogs, Elmira and Lefty.

Talk, talk, talk, talk, talk, talk, talk.

Fanny told Mary everything she could think of, everything she could put into words. Mary lightened Fanny's concern about Henry's episode earlier that day.

"So he's mad about his painting and he steps in the

dog dish? It wasn't Dinner's fault. *She* didn't step in the dog dish. It's not like she's a puppy and she's ruining stuff around the house. You know, like Nellie."

Fanny even told Mary about the boy in the red cap.

"Fanny!" Mary squealed. "If someone wanted their dog back, they would come to your house, knock on your door, and ask for their dog back. If anything," she said, her voice hushed and dramatic, "old Red Cap is probably madly in love with you and it has nothing to do with a dog. His love for you has been his secret for years—or at least weeks—but he's too bashful to tell you, so he follows you around, dreaming of the day he'll find the courage in his heart to introduce himself and let you know how he really feels about you." Mary closed her eyes and planted long, noisy kisses on the back of her hand and up her arm. She giggled. "Maybe Red Cap is Bruce Rankin."

"Thanks," said Fanny. "The biggest moron in school." She paused. "Really, though, it scared me when I thought he—whoever he is—might want Dinner back."

"Fanny, you worry too much. You, who always worries about failing exams and always gets A's. You, who used to be afraid of Mrs. Wagner's hollyhocks. No one's afraid of hollyhocks, but Fanny *Swann* is afraid of hollyhocks."

"Am not."

"Were too."

"Well, maybe." She had been. They were tall and

spikey and the most ugly purply red color she had ever seen and you never knew when Mrs. Wagner's shriveled old head would pop out from among them saying: "Girlie! Girlie! Want a treat?" just like the witch in "Hansel and Gretel." "I was afraid of *Mrs. Wagner*, not hollyhocks."

"I'll bet if you were walking alone and came upon a bed of them, you'd cross the street."

Fanny batted her eyelids. Maybe she would. She lifted her mug and swirled the dregs of her hot chocolate, peering at the remains as if they held the answers to every question ever asked.

"Betcha," Mary murmured.

"Auntie Fanny! Auntie Fanny!" Joey came galloping into the kitchen wearing his Batman cape made from a bath towel and a safety pin, and dragging a new, stuffed Mickey Mouse doll that was almost his size. Pea green crust decorated Joey's pale little upturned nose. His eyes were bubbles. He thrust the doll at Fanny. "Lookie!" he squeaked.

"Mickey Mouse. That's great."

"It's not Mickey Mouse," said Joey. "It's Catwoman. Meow."

"Oh, I see! She's nice."

Joey pointed out the diaper he had dressed her in and the Band-Aid on her nose. "No drips," he said. "Good kitty."

"Tom, the big-brother-jerk-of-the-world, put a Band-Aid on *Joey's* nose at my grandma's," Mary whispered, rolling her eyes. " 'Because it's always running,' he said. That's where Joey got the idea." She shook her head in disbelief.

"You, stay for dinner," Joey told Fanny. "You, too," he added, kissing Catwoman.

Fanny looked at her friend.

"Let's ask," said Mary.

Fanny stayed. And Mary walked her halfway home after supper. When she and Dinner were alone, Fanny imagined the painting that her father was working on. It was his biggest ever. A huge gathering of glassware, hit by brilliant light so that it sparkled in certain places, and even though it was clear glass, every color of the rainbow could be seen in the edges and reflections if you looked carefully. And if you looked even more carefully than that, near the cut-glass design in the most beautiful goblet, you would discover a portrait of the artist's daughter. And you would say, I wish I were that girl.

11

❄

Vacation ended for Fanny, but classes at the university weren't to resume for another three weeks, so while Fanny was at Eleanor Roosevelt Middle School and Ellen was at work, Henry and Dinner were alone in the house. Thoughts of what might be happening while she was away from home plagued Fanny throughout the day. She had ragged nails and a new habit of sucking on her knuckles to prove it. When the final bell would ring, Fanny would gather her things and race home. Sometimes she waited for Mary; sometimes she didn't. Usually, Dinner

was in the backyard, content, squirrels and birds occu-
pying her complete attention, or fast asleep on her afghan
by the radiator in the living room. (Fanny brought the
afghan down from her bedroom each morning and created
a comfortable nest for Dinner.) Their joyful reunion at
a quarter past three was a radiant point in Fanny's day.

Often, Henry had a complaint or two to register in a
sharp voice: *There is dog hair everywhere. An abundance.
Pinches of it like snowflakes. Enough to make a sweater. You
know where the vacuum cleaner is kept. After a new snowfall,
it's as if the yard were filled with land mines. Here's the trowel.
I don't want to have to be reminding you of your responsibilities.
She knocked a wineglass off the coffee table with her tail today.
I just thought you should know.*

When there were no complaints, it seemed to Fanny
that Henry was pleased with how his day had turned out
in respect to his painting. "I may be on to something,"
he said one afternoon. But just when Fanny would feel
relaxed about Dinner's future with her father, Henry
would become more formidable and touchy than ever.

So Fanny became vigilant. In a manner similar to that
with which she had protected Marie, Fanny began protecting Dinner. She set her alarm clock ten minutes earlier
each morning to pick up turds in the yard before school.
She moved Dinner's food and water dishes into the back
hall, completely out of harm's way. She vacuumed without being told, not only the rugs and floors, but the stairs,

radiators, and the bottom edge of the drapes as well. She anticipated the movement of Dinner's tail, watching Henry's wineglass on the coffee table before supper the way a new mother watches her infant, lurching forward at even the subtle suggestion of danger. On the Saturday after school had started again, she noticed wispy bullets of Dinner's hair on the bricks in the fireplace, and so she cleaned the fireplace entirely. I'm Cinderella, she thought as she swept the ashes. Fanny realized that a big, living, breathing dog is much harder to protect than a handmade paper doll that can be cradled in your hands or folded and concealed in a grown-up fist.

The weather kept changing. One day, the sky would be the color of lead, the next day, it would be forget-me-not blue, and following that, it might snow so hard that you wouldn't be able to see the sky. The wind would howl, the wind would stop. Cloudy, sunny, gloomy, bright, chilly, frigid, dry, damp. It occurred to Fanny that her father's moods were like the weather.

After it had been sunny for a couple of days, the snow on the roof melted and slender icicles formed along the gutter like the fringe on Henry and Ellen's bedspread. At the corner of the house, up high, where the downspout joined the gutter, a huge cluster of icicles hung. The gutter was overflowing with it. The cluster was weighty and multipointed, and it looked as though this isolated section of the house were wearing a majestic beard.

With the roof clear, Henry showed Fanny how to throw a tennis ball onto the roof so that it bounced down onto the lower roof above the screened back porch and then landed in the yard, to Dinner's great delight. After a few throws, Dinner caught the ball in midair nearly every time. Henry had come up with the idea that morning, he told Fanny, to avoid painting.

Fanny tried it. She had a good arm, and since Dinner had been with them it had grown stronger from playing fetch so often. On her first attempt, Fanny hit the bathroom window, but she readily got the hang of it.

"This is fun," she said gleefully.

Fanny continued to play after Henry had gone back inside the house.

It soon became a favorite game of Fanny and Dinner's, a daily activity as long as the roof was free of snow. Fanny even thought of a name for it—she called it roofball. "In the summer we can play it all day long," she told Dinner. Fanny held Dinner's ears up and made them dance.

One slushy afternoon, Fanny and Dinner's game of roofball was cut short. Within five minutes after they had begun playing, the back door sprung open, Henry's head appeared, and his voice sounded forth. "Please stop that. I can't concentrate." The door closed definitively like a period after his words.

Fanny curled her lip. "You taught it to me," she whispered, astonished. Impulsively, she threw the ball one last time. As hard as she could. It hit the chimney with a thud—directly where the chimney met the roof—and then rolled sluggishly into the gutter above the bathroom window. Oh, great, she thought. She was afraid to tell her father. Dinner ran back and forth along the edge of the house, her head held high, waiting for the ball to fall.

Days passed and the ball just sat there, hidden. Although Fanny kept many tennis balls as backups because Dinner occasionally lost them in the woods (she stored them in a canvas bag in her closet), she didn't dare take the chance of getting another one stuck in the gutter or ruining Henry's concentration. And that was the end of roofball.

Fanny couldn't fall asleep. It was a cold, noisy January night. The harder she tried, the more impossible the prospect became. She was so very close to sleep once, but the house cracked in the harsh winter air and her drowsiness quickly unraveled. She was wide awake again. Even her fan didn't help.

Dinner breathed like a horse and sighed like an elephant. Cars traveled by, two streets over. People arrived home and slammed their car doors. Keys turned in locks. Depending on how her head was angled on her pillow, Fanny could hear her blood flow. It seemed as though the whole world were spinning in the place where her brain was supposed to be.

Sleep, sleep, please fall asleep.

Her train of thought jumped with suddenness from one thing to another. From Dinner to Henry to Red Cap to Mary to Marie to Ellen to Nellie to Stuart Walker to the Snow Queen to Mary's young parents to old Mrs. Wagner and her hollyhocks to ice skates to the tennis ball stuck in the gutter.

Sleep, sleep, please fall asleep.

She wiggled her fingers directly in front of her eyes, staring at them for so long that they no longer looked like fingers. In the darkened room, they looked like ugly little things, nimble sea creatures that weren't a part of her. Restlessly, she moved from her stomach to her side to her back, wondering if lying on her stomach would keep her breasts from developing.

Sleep, sleep, please fall asleep.

She closed her eyes and imagined skating a figure eight. Her eyes moved up, around, over, down, up, around, over, down. Was a figure eight, lying down, a symbol for infinity or eternity? She couldn't remember.

Eternity infinity, eternity infinity, eternity infinity.

Sleep, sleep, please fall asleep.

That night, Fanny coined a new word, her word, a combination of eternity and infinity: internity. Internity was her name for the time of night when even the softest noise is loud, when you want to sleep and you can't, when your mind is racing and it won't stop, and it feels as though morning will never come.

Internity internity internity.

Sleep, sleep, please fall asleep.

There was only one thing to do. Fanny crept over to Dinner's bed. Dinner stirred; she licked Fanny's face. Fanny reached for her comforter from the foot of her bed and dragged it along the floor. She wrapped herself snugly and curled around her dog, her right arm circling Dinner and her left arm resting diagonally across Dinner's chest. Her right hand cupped the crown of Dinner's head and her left hand was tucked between Dinner's leg and belly. With her tags jingling, Dinner gave Fanny one last lick out of the side of her mouth. The holey, dove-colored afghan was warm and smelled so good to Fanny, so unlike her own bed, like the earth. Trying to match her breathing with Dinner's, Fanny shut her eyes.

Sleep, sleep, please fall asleep.

Internity finally ended. Fanny finally fell asleep.

School was over for the day and Fanny was running late. After her last class, she walked swiftly to the library, darting in and out among the students, clutching her books to her chest, twisting this way and that way to get through the crowd without knocking into anyone. In the library near the checkout desk, the most massive diction- ary Fanny had ever seen lay open. It was even thicker than the maroon leather-bound dictionary that her parents kept in the den. Fanny searched for her word. Internity. She located the page where it should have appeared; the entries jumped from internist to internment, just like the dictionary at home. Good, she thought smugly, it really, truly is my own word.

At her locker, she decided which books to bring home, loaded her backpack, and threw on her coat. She paused, looking into the small, dim rectangular cave, wondering how one goes about getting a word known to many people, how one gets a word into a dictionary. For now, she would keep it to herself. A photograph of Dinner was taped to the inside of her locker door. The photograph, taken on Christmas morning, showed Dinner sporting a loopy green bow from a present, her tongue lolling. It reminded Fanny to hurry up, to get home to see what Dinner and Henry were doing.

Because the locker door was still open, Fanny didn't see him at first. When she slammed it shut, he startled her.

It was a boy she barely knew. A big-eared, spindly boy with mussed hair. A boy named Timothy Hill.

He didn't say anything, so Fanny whispered, "Hi."

"Hi," he answered shyly.

Fanny's expression conveyed what she was thinking: What do you want?

The boy's hands were jammed deeply into his coat pockets. He shifted his weight from foot to foot, watching the ribbons of dirty water on the floor and only stealing peeks at Fanny. "I, uh, don't know if you know, but my name is Timothy Hill," he said slowly and quietly.

"I know."

"And you're Fanny Swann," he said. "Dumb," he added in a whisper, rolling his eyes, obviously embarrassed by his remark.

Fanny started walking down the long hallway. She needed to get home.

Timothy Hill shuffled along sideways to keep up. "I have something of yours," he told her.

Fanny stopped. "What?"

"I found it on Christmas morning. In my backyard, caught in a bittersweet bush." Timothy Hill pulled a crumpled piece of paper, some string, and a deflated balloon out of his pocket.

Fanny gasped. "Give me that," she said. It was the note she had written and released in the middle of the night, the night her father had stayed away. She snatched the note, string, and balloon from his hand. "Did you read it?" she asked. "Of course you read it."

Timothy Hill nodded.

"It's none of your business, you know," she said, fully aware that it wasn't his fault at all that this had happened, but hers. She unfolded the note and reread it. *At this very moment I don't understand my father and would like a new one. If you're interested, please reply.* Her initials were there, plain as could be, and so was her address. "It was a joke, anyway. I didn't really mean it. About my father." Of course she had meant it, but it was a matter of privacy that concerned her now. Oh, how she regretted what she had done. What good could possibly have come from sending a silly, impulsive message off by way of a balloon? "So how did you know F. S. was me?"

Timothy Hill blushed vividly. His cheeks were bright pink. "It was kind of like an adventure. I walked by the address on the paper and I saw you on your porch. That's when I knew you were F. S. I even checked on you a couple of times, you know, because of what the note said. I saw you playing with a dog and you seemed happy, and I saw you skating with two people who I think were your parents and you were all laughing, so I figured you were okay. But if—"

"You can't tell anyone about this," Fanny instructed urgently, trying her best to sound forceful.

"I won't."

"Promise?"

"Promise."

"Now you have to tell me something about you," she insisted. "Something that you don't want anyone to know."

Timothy Hill shrugged and blushed again. His face puckered. Fanny almost thought that she could hear him pondering this, wheels turning and turning in his head, synapses firing. Seconds passed like minutes before he reached into his backpack and lovingly drew out a red knitted cap. The cap had a long braid with a tassel at the end and earflaps decorated with white snowflakes. "I knit," he said. "I made this."

Muscles twitched in Fanny's neck, and she felt a tickle at the back of her throat. *"You,"* she said loudly. *"You're* Red Cap."

Timothy Hill looked completely confused. "I don't wear it around school. I'd probably get teased. My older brother calls me Baby Hat when I wear it."

"You don't want to take my dog. You don't even *know* my dog." Fanny's voice cracked. "Thank you. Oh, thank you." She took a deep breath. "I've got to run," she said in parting.

Bewildered, Timothy Hill was left in the middle of the hallway, holding his hat tightly in both hands. "But . . . wait . . ."

"It's a long story," Fanny called back over her shoulder. "Maybe I'll tell you someday!"

If she were Mary Dibble, she would have been shrieking with joy the entire way home. But she was Fanny Swann, and so she held her joy deep inside her like a secret that crept out in a constant smile, a smile that burst across her face from ear to ear.

With one less thing to worry about, Fanny celebrated. She fixed hot chocolate for herself with three jumbo marshmallows, and she presented Dinner with three dog biscuits. "For you, ma'am," she said playfully in a silly British accent. Then her voice returned to normal. "Red Cap's not going to take you away," she told Dinner.

"He's just a kid at school." She closed her eyes and let the truth of her statement sink in.

Because she was so happy, Fanny was eager to see her parents. She didn't plan on telling them about Timothy Hill; she simply wanted her family near. But Ellen was still at work and Henry hadn't come down from his studio. While she waited, Fanny pretended to be a dog.

She dropped to her knees; her hands turned into paws. Clumsily, she padded up to Dinner and they sniffed each other. Fanny tried different things—grooming herself, kicking her leg out, imagining a long, dense, golden tail with beautiful streaks of red. She wiggled her rear and her tail swayed gracefully, collecting dirt and dust from the kitchen floor. Her ears grew, becoming soft and flexible. Whiskers sprouted beneath her nose and across her cheeks. From someplace low in her chest came a muffled growl. Her nostrils quivered. Then, with her head cocked, she began to pant.

Fanny was still panting when Henry entered the kitchen.

Henry clicked his tongue disapprovingly. "Fanny," he said, "act your age." He shot her a look that completely diminished her.

A fraction of a second was as long as she could keep her eyes on him. But in that time she noticed one long hair in his eyebrow that had strayed from the rest in a twisty fashion like a bolt of lightning.

A girl again, a daughter, she rose silently and walked

away. She fought back tears until she was in her room, flopped on her bed. And then the tears streamed down her face and onto her hands and pillow. Almost immediately, Dinner was beside her. Her nose nudged Fanny's hands from her face, and she licked the tears.

"I love you," said Fanny.

Dinner nuzzled closer and closer.

"Why do I act so dumb sometimes?"

With her head buried in Dinner's neck, Fanny breathed in Dinner's smell. Combined with her usual doggy smell was a lingering hint of turpentine.

Fanny sat up with a start. "You weren't in his studio, were you?" she asked, alarmed. "Don't ever go in there," she instructed Dinner. "Ever, ever, ever."

Their eyes fastened together.

If only you could talk to me, Fanny thought. If only you could tell me what goes on all day.

12

❄

Fanny had two secrets—internity and Timothy Hill. In the back of her English notebook she wrote a definition for internity, copying the format of a real dictionary:

> **in·ter·ni·ty**\(ĭn-tûr´nĭ-tē)\ *n* [created by Fanny Swann of Madison, WI]: The dismal, endless time of night when one cannot fall asleep.

She hoped that she had divided the word into syllables correctly and that her definition sounded professional. It had taken Fanny days to come up with something that pleased her. She also doodled knitted caps with earflaps and tassels. Pages and pages of them. Another page in the same notebook was filled from top to bottom and from side to side with Fanny's last name alternating with Timothy's last name. Swann Hill Swann Hill Swann Hill Swann. When she wrote the names, Fanny tried to fashion the capital S in Swann to resemble a swan, and she constructed the capital H in Hill with a rise like a hill. Her skill improved and her creativity blossomed by the end of the page.

We both have last names you can draw, she thought, somehow thrilled by this discovery.

Since their brief, confusing introduction, Fanny and Timothy began running into each other in the hallways at school rather frequently. Why is it, she wondered, that after you meet someone you tend to see them everywhere? Fanny would smile politely at him, and Timothy would blush and grin as if he had just done something slightly devilish. His eyes would bounce about like popcorn popping, then slide back to Fanny. They'd both turn their heads awkwardly after they passed, looking, looking one last time.

"I think he likes you," Mary said to Fanny. They were standing at Fanny's locker before classes one morning. Timothy had just walked by. "Have you noticed the way he smirks at you?"

"What do you mean?" Fanny could feel the color in her cheeks rise, so she tipped her head forward so that it was hidden inside her open locker.

"You know what I mean," said Mary. "Hey, look at me. Come on." Mary grabbed Fanny's chin and turned her head around. "Oh, my God," she said. "You're in love."

"Shut up."

"You are."

"Am not."

"Are too."

Fanny wasn't ready to explain that Timothy Hill was Red Cap. And she couldn't bring herself to say that no boy had ever paid attention to her before, and that a goofy smile was far better than no smile. She also couldn't say how it made her feel. She didn't know the words.

"He's got a chipped tooth, you know," said Mary. "And a space like David Letterman's," she added, thrusting her fingernail between her two front teeth.

Fanny closed her locker door and stuck her tongue out at Mary.

Mary stuck her tongue out at Fanny.

They brushed their shoulders together, giggling, and walked through patches of sunlight to their first class.

"How old do I have to be to go on a date?" Fanny asked her mother as she unloaded the dishwasher. She hugged a hot, clean platter to her chest and leaned against the sink.

Ellen had just hung up the telephone. Fanny had been waiting.

"Oh, I don't know," Ellen answered, picking at her cuticle. "Twenty-five."

"No, really."

"It depends on what you mean by a date."

"Mom."

"Eighteen."

"Mo-om," groaned Fanny.

"All right, all right, sixteen . . . fifteen . . . *fourteen?*" Ellen fingered the end of her ponytail, twirling it. "Why?"

"Just wondering," said Fanny.

"Just wondering about what?" Henry asked. He had carried an assortment of dirty mugs down from his studio. He rinsed them and set them in the sink.

"Nothing," Fanny said at last, and she went about her work.

Henry and Ellen had gone to a movie. They had asked Fanny to go with them, but she decided to stay home. Henry had been particularly moody all day—early in the morning before Fanny had left for school, in the afternoon when she had returned, and throughout supper, when he seemed distracted to the point of being elusive. Fanny thought that being alone with Ellen, out of the house, away from his work, might be good for him. Maybe it would take his mind off his painting. Henry and Ellen could talk the way Fanny imagined parents talked when their children weren't around. And furthermore, *she'd* get a break from *him.*

Fanny wasn't fearful about being by herself in the house at night any longer. This was a change that had come about since Dinner had entered her life. It was a nice change, and recently Fanny had been anticipating *other* changes, changes that would take place when she turned thirteen in March. She would be a teenager. That in itself would be an accomplishment. Even the sound of it—*thirteen*—was exhilarating. With any luck, the physical changes she had been waiting for would begin to show. And she was certain that there would be invisible, inside things that would change as well. Things inside her body, things inside her head. I'll grow into my nose, she thought. I'll become elegant. My life will be different.

With Dinner right beside her, Fanny locked the door after her parents left. An ancient gray scarf of Ellen's was hanging out of the wooden bin near the front door like a saggy elephant trunk. Fanny tugged it, freed it from the bin, and casually wound it around her neck, throwing one end over her shoulder. "When I'm thirteen," she said with a lofty air, jutting her chin out, "I'll be . . . be . . ." She was searching for the perfect adjective.

Dinner barked, a small, short, clear bark.

"Exactly. I couldn't have said it better," remarked Fanny. "Hey, I have an idea." She stepped back to the bin, and balancing on one leg, bent over, and rummaged with intent. It took some effort and she practically fell into the bin, but Fanny managed to retrieve a striped stocking cap, a lint-covered beret, and a pair of fuzzy white earmuffs. "This will be fun," she said, slapping her thigh so Dinner would follow her. Dinner's nails clipped rhythmically on the floor.

The living room was dim. The light from the end table lamp was honey colored, yet pallid, and they sat in the wan apron it cast. After choosing the earmuffs, Fanny gently slipped them onto Dinner's head.

Dinner acted as though the earmuffs were a natural part of her body, an extension of her own ears. And Fanny marveled at that. Dinner was so gentle, so good-natured, so amiable. Recently, at the Dibbles', Joey had leaped onto Dinner's back, encircling her neck with his arms like a vise and clamping his legs to her belly. Rocking up and down on her to urge her to move forward, he chirped, "She thinks she's the Batmobile! Vroom! Vroom!"

Without a complaint, Dinner endured it all, while miraculously maintaining a look of modest nobility. Even when it got a bit rough, she stood solidly and remained calm, although her head drooped off to the side and she cast her eyes downward in such a way that it caused Fanny's heart to ache.

"You're the best," Fanny praised.

With the earmuffs on, Fanny pretended that Dinner was her mother. She told Dinner to lie down, and she arranged her front legs so that they were spread wide. "There," Fanny said. "You're Mom doing yoga."

Next came the beret. Set at a jaunty slant, it transformed Dinner into Henry. "You have to scowl," Fanny said. "Puff your cheeks, Dinner, like you do when you seem sad." The beret slid off Dinner's head; Fanny placed it back, right on top where it wouldn't fall. "Hi, Dad," she said. "I like you better as a dog." Fanny cranked her head around so that she faced a small framed photograph of Henry on the bookshelf. "Just kidding."

In the striped stocking cap, Dinner was Timothy Hill. "I know it's not exactly right, but it'll do. It's nice," she said, straightening it, making it secure. "Did you know we both have last names you can draw?" She cleared her throat. "Oh, by the way, I saw a hockey stick in your locker when I walked by the other day. Would you like to play sometime?"

Dinner stretched and stretched, yawned and stretched.

"You are such a good sport," Fanny complimented Dinner. "And I like *you* best as a dog, too." She ripped the stocking cap off Dinner's head, scooped up the earmuffs and beret, unwound the scarf from around her neck, skipped to the hallway, and flung it all into the bin. Dinner stayed where she was, watching Fanny intently every second.

Starting with an ear massage, Fanny stroked Dinner enthusiastically. And Dinner loved it, rolling onto her side, seeking more attention. She shaped herself into an S. Fanny kept at it, raking her fingers through Dinner's thick fur.

After about ten minutes, Fanny clapped her hands to her legs. "That's all," she said. "Time to call Mary." Her hands left dark, dirty prints on her beige jeans. She turned her hands over in her lap. Her palms were filthy from petting Dinner. Either it was charcoal from her father's studio, she reasoned, or plain old dirt. She considered this, glancing from her hands to Dinner.

Fervently she chose to believe that it was dirt, and nothing more. Not charcoal. Simply dirt.

Several days later when Fanny came home from school, the front door was locked. This wouldn't have been unusual if it had been a Tuesday or a Thursday—the days Henry taught—but it was a Wednesday. On Wednesdays, Henry was nearly always at home.

Fanny didn't think much about this as she unlocked the door. Her ears were straining, listening for the sound of Dinner's tags.

Nothing.

Smiling, she called Dinner's name in a sweet singsong

voice, picturing her fast asleep on her afghan near the fireplace. When Fanny entered the living room, Dinner was nowhere to be seen. And neither was the afghan.

The missing afghan was what caused her to panic. As part of her morning routine, she had brought the afghan down before she had left for school. She knew she had done this, as surely as she knew her name. If Henry had taken Dinner for a walk (which he rarely did), the afghan would still be there. Automatically, Fanny flew through the house room by room, shouting for Dinner and trying to convince herself to calm down, that there was nothing to worry about.

The house was unbearably empty.

Only one other time in her life had Fanny been alone in the house and felt it so. Approximately five years earlier, on a rainy spring afternoon, she had been taking a bath. Her parents had been in the living room, reading. Henry's music—something classical—was playing on the stereo. It streamed in through the floor and walls to Fanny, where she lay in the tub, up to her chin in silky water, encircled by lemony bubbles. Rain tapped against the roof. When she was done with her bath, she toweled off, dressed, and went down to be with her parents. "I'm back," she said, hopping off the last step joyfully. But no one was there. The music still played—strings, she remembered, snapping, mounting. Her parents' books were strewn across the sofa as if the people reading them had left in a hurry, or worse, had been snatched away, and Fanny knew that the world had ended. She checked the house from top to bottom before she sat in a corner and burst into tears. She hugged her knees and swayed back and forth.

In a matter of minutes, the screen door slammed and they were standing above her. "What's wrong? What happened? Why are you crying?" they asked, crouching down to her, Henry's knees cracking.

"I didn't know ... what happened to you," she said, trying to catch her breath. "I thought something ... *bad* happened." She sniffled. "Or you left ... me."

Ellen hugged Fanny. "There, there," she soothed. "I realized that the rain had stopped, and through the window I felt the sun creeping back," she said. "I wanted to see if there was a rainbow, so we went out to the corner, sweetie. We were just standing on the corner and only for a few minutes. If you hurry, it might still be there," Ellen said, motioning with her hand.

Relief rushed through Fanny like a storm. She caught her breath. And the three of them scurried out to see the rainbow. Fanny stared at it until her eyes hurt, until the rainbow was gone.

"Next time we step outside for *any* reason," said Henry, "we'll check with you first, your majesty."

She knew that he was trying to make a joke because his voice was light and he squeezed her hand as he said it, but his words made her feel ashamed of how she had acted, and she pulled her hand away.

Now, shaking her head, Fanny realized how frivolous the rainbow incident seemed. She tried to breathe the way her mother had taught her. Yoga breathing. Slow and deep. She decided to call her mother at work to see if she knew anything of Henry and Dinner's whereabouts. As she reached for the telephone, Fanny noticed a note and a magnet lying beneath the kitchen table. They had fallen from the refrigerator, she guessed. She picked the note up, turned it in her hand. The note said:

> I'm at Stuart's.
> I'll be back soon.
> I took Dinner with me.
> Henry/Dad

When Fanny read this, the only thing she could think of was Stuart Walker's comment, early on New Year's Day: ". . . if you can't handle *this* dog, give me a call. I'd take her in a heartbeat."

Was the afghan missing because Henry had taken Dinner to Stuart's house for good? Had Dinner been in Henry's studio, messing things up, interfering with his work?

Fanny ran to the coat hooks in the front hall; Dinner's leash was gone. She ran to the back hall; Dinner's food and water dishes were missing. She opened the cupboard; the box of dog biscuits was no longer there, and neither was the plastic pouch of rawhide bones.

Now Fanny felt real panic. She took the steps two at a time, up to the second floor, and spun around the corner. The house was so dry she received a shock when she switched on the light for the narrow flight of stairs that led up to Henry's attic studio. "Ouch," she whispered. She hadn't been in his studio since before Christmas, since the night of his birthday party when she looked for him there.

With great hesitancy, she opened the door. It creaked and creaked. Without even stepping into the studio she could see charcoal dog prints running chaotically across the floor. Some were clearly defined, others were smudgy black moons. And wedged between the wall and one of the legs of the cart on which Henry piled his tubes of paint was Dinner's squeaky rubber snowman toy.

Fanny tiptoed to the snowman and disengaged it. She had been looking for it for days—under her bed, in her closet, out in the yard. Checking here had never crossed her mind. She turned abruptly to leave, and as she did, she was confronted with the painting on her father's easel.

The painting was large for Henry—four feet by three feet. It was currently in a grisaille stage, an underpainting in shades of gray, waiting to be glazed with color. The composition was crowded, vases and bowls and jars bleeding off the panel in every direction. Fanny recognized some of the vessels; they were the ones she had given Henry for Christmas. But what stopped her and stunned her was a quick, feathery rendering of a dog that covered about a quarter of the panel. It was incongruous with the rest of the panel, an afterthought. But there was no question about it. Surely it was Dinner. Henry had captured her perfectly—the way she tended to lie with her front paw curved oddly, sticking out like a number seven. The lines that described her body were ashen and washy. The rendering of Dinner, in itself, would have been fine, but the mark of a thick, black X had been made over her, blotting her out, canceling her.

X.

It was as if Henry had planned it all as a game, a hunt, similar to the wonderful birthday hunts he had orchestrated when Fanny was a child. She'd follow simple clues from room to room, ending at the linen closet or the laundry room, which would be filled with presents and balloons and candy. Once, the mysterious directions led to the guest room, which was decorated in a circus motif and jammed with whispering friends anticipating the moment to shout "Happy Birthday!" and throw confetti. Her cake was as big as a bed pillow that year and shaped like a lion.

Those hunts were joyful and exciting; this was a cruel joke.

The big black X said it all so simply: Henry had gotten rid of Dinner.

Fanny squinched into the corner and started to cry. And then she said the words out loud, words that she had thought before but never spoken, even when Henry had told her that Nellie had to go: "I hate him."

13

After she had composed herself enough so that her voice wasn't shaking, Fanny called her mother at work. "Do you know anything about Dad going to Stuart Walker's house?" she asked.

"No," said Ellen. "He didn't mention it to me this morning. He was in his studio when I left. I heard him humming behind the closed door, so maybe, just maybe, he's gotten over this block."

Fanny was using the stationary phone in the kitchen.

She wove the cord through her fingers, then poked her pinkie through the coils. "Where was Dinner?"

"This morning?"

"Yeah."

"Following me around, as usual, while I was getting dressed. She was lying on her afghan when I left. Why?"

"Dunno."

"Fanny, you sound funny. Are you all right?"

Sniffle.

"Fanny," said Ellen, "are you crying?"

"Kind of."

"What's wrong?"

As clearly and slowly as she could, Fanny told her mother what she had discovered when she had arrived home from school.

"Did you call Stuart?" asked Ellen, her voice steady.

"I thought I'd call you first. I thought maybe you'd know something."

"Sit tight," said Ellen. "I'll call Stuart and then I'll call you right back. And don't worry. Bye."

They hung up. And in the silence that followed, the day's events fleshed themselves out in Fanny's mind: Henry had been painting, happily, until Dinner entered his studio. Dinner distracted him. Her tail swept charcoal dust throughout the room and knocked things over. She pranced and dodged about, wanting to play, inviting Henry to join her, pressing her squeaky rubber snowman toy with her paw. Henry's impatience mounted until he reached the point . . .

The telephone rang. Fanny answered it before the first ring was completed. "Mom?"

"The answering machine is on," said Ellen. "I left a message for your father to call home."

Fanny sighed. "What am I going to do? I know he took her away." If she wasn't careful, she was going to cry again. She closed her eyes and willed herself to be stoic.

"He wouldn't do that," Ellen told her solemnly.

"He did it before."

Now it was Ellen who sighed. "That was different," she said, but her voice wasn't nearly as steady as it had been. "I've got one phone call to make for work, and then I'll be right home. Okay?"

"Okay."

"Don't worry," Ellen reassured her. "We'll wait together."

A car door slammed and Fanny ran to the window.
Empty street.

A dog bayed far, far away and Fanny opened the front door.

The wind?

Fanny sat by the phone, anticipating its ringing. She even lifted the receiver off its cradle once.

Only the dial tone.

Why was it, Fanny wondered, that lately she was always waiting for her father? Waiting for him to come to his party. Waiting for him to return after he had disappeared. Waiting for him to approve of her Christmas gift. Waiting for him to get on with his painting. Waiting for him to overcome a bad mood. Waiting for the world to fall into place around him. Waiting, waiting, waiting.

Because she didn't know where else to go, Fanny shuffled to her room. She tried to review the facts a thousand different ways—changing this, changing that—but she always arrived at the same conclusion: Dinner is gone.

The days were lengthening and the sunlight that brightened Fanny's room had a different quality to it than even a few days earlier. As a means of comfort, a need for the familiar, Fanny opened her file cabinet and surveyed her possessions. The light caught the bottle of dragées and the glint it made caught Fanny's eye. She picked up the bottle and read the list of ingredients. Sugar, cornstarch, gelatin, acetic acid, and silver. She figured that it was the silver that made them nonedible. She poured some of the silvery beads into her hand. They rolled into the creases of her palm, and Fanny held them there until some of the silver rubbed off onto her skin.

The idea to crush them between her fingers struck her, and she tried it, with no success. The hard little balls shot out from between her fingers and ricocheted around the room. Finally, and with great effort, she was able to pulverize a bunch of them with her boot on the floor. Squatting, she contemplated the result—a tiny pile of dust, like sugar or snow.

Thinking of "The Snow Queen," Fanny pretended that the dust was magic. If she ate the dust, it would prick her heart and force her into a frozen sleep. And wouldn't her father be sorry then?

Ever so slowly, Fanny licked her finger, stuck it into the pile, then put her finger into her mouth. The powder tasted faintly sweet, almost like nothing. Fanny blew the rest of the powder away, and she replaced the bottle of dragées in the file cabinet.

She removed Marie when she fitted the dragées back into the drawer. Marie. Flimsy, handmade paper doll. The hours and hours of fretting over her survival seemed like such a waste of time to Fanny. The tissue paper that was wrapped around her fell away. Fanny tenderly bounced the doll in her hand. And then suddenly, as if by doing it she would somehow increase the chances of a miracle for Dinner, Fanny tore Marie's arms and legs from her body and wadded them. Without pause, she ripped the body into the smallest pieces she could and threw the whole tattered mess into the wastebasket.

And she continued to wait.

"Dinner! Oh, Dinner!"
When Fanny saw Dinner's head in the window of

Henry's car, her scalp tingled with relief, a sensation that swooped through her, lingering in her fingertips and toes for minutes. She was at the curbside, her hand working the door handle, before Henry had clicked the ignition off. Dinner's wet nose left wavy smudges diagonally across the window. The door flew open and Dinner leaped from the car. Dinner knocked Fanny over onto the crusty snow in the front yard, licking her excitedly.

"I thought you were gone," Fanny said to Dinner, hiding her face in Dinner's fur. "Forever." The corners of Fanny's eyes were welling with tears.

Surprisingly, it had started to snow; the sun still shone low in the sky. Flakes as big as moths were falling.

The idea of Dinner's being taken away hit Fanny all over again, and she broke into tears quietly.

"What's the matter?" asked Henry, hurrying around the car with rolls of paper under his arms like sticks.

Fanny picked herself up off the ground and blinked. She peered at her father through the veil of snow. "I thought you had taken Dinner away. Her afghan and all her special things were missing."

"Oh, Fanny, I'm sorry that that's what you were thinking. I took Dinner to Stuart's with me. That's all. I left you a note."

"I know." But it hadn't been clear to her.

"In, in, in," Henry said, coaxing Fanny along with a nod. "You'll get sick out here. It's freezing."

She had no coat on, no mittens, no hat, and suddenly she was aware of the cold.

"Here," said Henry, "take these and I'll go get Dinner's belongings." He handed the rolls of paper to Fanny and went back to the car.

Just then Ellen drove up to the house. Fanny watched her parents from the front window. They talked by the cars, their hands fluttering, fingers pointing. They unloaded Henry's car, divided Dinner's belongings, and, their arms brimming (with other things, too—Ellen's purse and Henry's satchel), lugged it all up the sidewalk.

"There you are," Ellen said to Fanny as she stamped into the house, shaking off snow. She came toward Fanny, leaving mazes of slush on the floor from her boots. Ellen embraced Fanny, breathing into her hair. "Everything's okay now."

Fanny wasn't so sure yet. "I still don't understand," she said.

Henry lightly rubbed her shoulder. "I'll show you," he said merrily. "I'll show you."

She was resistant to his touch.

Holding one of the rolls of paper as a baton, Henry directed them to the dining room table. He unfurled the roll. It was a charcoal drawing of the interior of a room, done very loosely, lacking the clarity of Henry's finished paintings. The focal point was a table. A cloth was draped over the tabletop, cascading off one end of it, landing in folds on the floor. Broken dishes and what looked like scraps of food were scattered across the table. And beneath the table, fading into shadow, was Dinner. Triangles—pieces of plates and teacups—surrounded her.

There were more drawings, all of Dinner, under the table or beside the chair from Henry's studio, or lost amid his collection of pots and bowls and vases.

"I've been trying to incorporate Dinner into my painting," said Henry. "I've been doing these preliminary drawings for weeks. But I couldn't get her to remain still long enough for my needs. I'd forgotten how difficult it is to draw a living thing. So today I took her to Stuart's to have her photographed for reference. He shot about a dozen rolls of film of her in various positions." Henry paused, then stroked his chin with a charcoal-smeared finger, leaving a dark cleft behind. "I've been so bored with my work recently, and concerned about having enough for the show in New York. I didn't tell you sooner because I wasn't convinced it would prove successful. I think—*hope*—that this is the breakthrough I've been waiting for."

Henry let his attention drift back to Fanny. "I took her afghan and toys and dishes with me to make her feel more at home."

It was all so obvious to Fanny now. Why Dinner had smelled of turpentine. Why she had been dirtied with charcoal dust. Even the X on the sketch of Dinner on

Henry's easel made sense. Henry had only been indicating his frustration. The picture hadn't been right. And, of course, Henry had taken Dinner to Stuart Walker's because he was a professional photographer.

"Look at these," Henry said, pulling some Polaroid photographs out of his jacket pocket and handing them to Fanny. "Stuart also shot these today. I'll use them until he develops the others."

Although she tried not to show it, Fanny was exceedingly interested in the photographs. She glanced at them nonchalantly when in fact she wanted to study them carefully. She loved them. They were wonderful: Dinner on her afghan. Dinner nearly concealed by houseplants. Dinner curled up into a tight heap like a cinnamon bun. Dinner extended along the floor as if she were flying, her plumelike tail arced behind her. Dinner sitting with her head tilting off to one side and her gaze tilting off, too, little commas of white outlining her eyes. Every angle. All sides. Awake, asleep.

"She's a star," Ellen said, as she took her turn with the photographs.

"Dinner was great today," Henry remarked, rolling up his drawings and snapping one of the rubber bands that bound them. "Great, great, great. I can't wait to get working."

"What a relief, huh?" Ellen whispered as she slipped past Fanny to the kitchen. "Hooray for small miracles."

Throughout supper, Henry was blissful and Ellen was placid. And Fanny? Fanny's heart was thrashing, but she tried to sit and eat prettily and politely. Her father didn't understand how upset she had been. A hole had been knocked into her life—permanently, she had thought— and he seemed barely to notice. Fanny cleaned her plate, folded her napkin into a tepee, placed it on the table, and asked to be excused.

"Visiting hours tonight?" Henry's voice came from behind the closed door.

"I guess," Fanny mumbled. She was sitting cross-legged on the floor with Dinner, her nightgown stretched tightly over her knees. The taut, shallow valley she had formed was sprinkled with pieces of Marie. They reminded Fanny of wilted petals. She picked up a number of them, released them from the height of her chin, and observed them as they dropped to her lap.

Henry sat on Fanny's bed, sinking down, down into the mattress. The springs made a mournful sound.

Watching him, Fanny had the feeling that she was rising slowly through deep water. And then, before he even spoke, she felt a strong sensation of déjà vu, as if she had been in this very spot, beside her dog, looking up to her pale-eyed, white-haired father, who sat on her bed with the stature of God.

"You were quiet at supper," said Henry.

"Oh," was all she managed to say through a weak, close-lipped smile.

"You're still mad at me," Henry said slowly and thoughtfully, without a trace of his professor voice coming through. "I'm the first to admit that you've had good cause to be mad, many times, but today was no one's fault. I had absolutely no intention of taking Dinner away, so how could I have guessed that that's what you would be thinking?"

Fanny shrugged.

"Your mother told me how upset you were when you came home from school. And for that I'm truly sorry." Henry paused, waiting, it seemed, for Fanny to say something. When she didn't, he added, "Dinner's really sacked out, isn't she? We played a lot of ball at Stuart's house. With all the land they've got, it was great fun." He paused again. "Well . . . at least there was a happy ending." He stood up to leave. The sigh that flew from his pursed lips was a sigh of defeat.

There was a gnawing inside Fanny's stomach as if a trapped mouse were trying fiercely to work its way out. If only she could say the things she was thinking. What an impossible task! First, she would have to find the right words to describe how she felt, and then she would have to say them in such a way that they wouldn't make him hate her, or, worse, cause him to give up on her, ignore her, compel him to leave again, this time for good.

"You always have to have everything just so, and I'm always trying to make things exactly the way you want them to be," she blurted out. "I always feel like I have to cover my tracks. Why can't I just be a kid? And why can't Dinner just be a dog?" She went on, "At Mary's, the dogs go on the furniture and no one cares. Jackets are always on the floor by the front door and it's all right. Dishes pile up in the sink and it's not a big deal."

Wincing, Henry squatted, his back touching Fanny's bed. The joints in his knees and hips were straining greatly; they made the noises to prove it. "I know that I can be a difficult person, but the bottom line is that I love you. No matter what. Everyone has their problems—even fussy adults." Henry chuckled and smoothed Fanny's comforter. "Maybe Mary complains to *her* parents: 'Fanny's house is always so clean and it's all right. There are never toys and coats and newspapers strewn about the house and it's not a big deal.'"

Fanny swallowed, ignoring his joke. "You don't under-*stand* me sometimes," she whispered, her voice changing sharply as her emotions rose. "I'm *always* worrying that you're going to take something away from me."

"Nellie," said Henry. "Nellie was a special case. I made a mistake, but that doesn't mean it's going to happen again."

Fanny bent over to kiss Dinner, inching closer to her. "How can I be sure?"

"You just have to be."

Fanny looked at her father expectantly.

"Listen to me," said Henry. "You just have to trust me," he told her loudly and clearly and steadily as if it could only be the truth.

Fanny felt a chill. With her hands in her lap, she spread her fingers and silently counted the things that Henry had taken away from her and the things that had seemed in jeopardy at one time or another. Marie. Nellie. Dinner. Roofball—which he had taught her, then scolded her for playing. Her antique-store coat with the fake leopard-skin collar—"I'll buy you a new coat, no matter how much it costs. That thing is awful. You look deprived in it."

"What are you doing?" Henry wanted to know.

"Nothing." Then Fanny collected a handful of the pieces of paper that had once been Marie, her beloved doll. "You tried to take *her* away."

"What?"

"Marie," she stated, raising her cupped hand, tipping it toward her father. "Every week you tried to take her away."

"I don't understand," said Henry. One of his eyebrows rose and fell like a wave. "What do you mean?"

Fanny described who Marie was, how much she had meant to Fanny, and how Fanny had tried to hide her week after week after week.

"I don't remember her at all," said Henry. "I *do* remember Stupid Hunts, but I don't remember Marie."

"It doesn't matter, she's just a doll. *Was* just a doll."

"Did Dinner do that?" Henry pointed to the scraps of paper.

"No. I did."

"Why?"

"It's hard to explain." Fanny smiled vaguely. "But I guess it worked."

"Oh," said Henry, obviously not at all certain what Fanny had meant by her last comment.

"You *really* don't remember her?"

"Not at all," answered Henry, shaking his head.

Good, thought Fanny. She believed him.

Dinner was lying as flat as a blanket, her tail tucked beneath her. Father and daughter petted her simultaneously. Their fingers grazed ever so slightly.

Then Henry patted Fanny's knee. He hoisted himself up off the floor, and just as he reached the threshold, Fanny spoke again.

"Sometimes I'm afraid of you," she whispered, her voice barely audible. It was the closest she could come to summing it all up. She didn't want him to respond. She had just needed to say it.

Her father turned and walked slowly back to her. An expression of recognition rippled across his face. And Fanny noticed something shift in his eyes. He hesitated briefly. "Sometimes," he said quietly, almost sweetly, "*I'm* afraid of *you*."

Fanny squinted at her father in disbelief. "You are?"

He grabbed her hand and kissed it. A fleeting peck, short and quick.

Fanny rose by grabbing on to his arms and pulling herself up with all her might, the tiny fragments of Marie fluttering to the floor all around them.

They hugged.

"Are you okay?" he asked.

She nodded.

And suddenly, in his arms she felt safe, strangely so, because her father, strong, formidable Henry, needed to be hugged just as much as if not more than she did. And she was certain, as certain as she was of anything, that Dinner was safe, too.

Part Three

Within

14

❄

One genial February afternoon when Henry came home from teaching on campus, his canvas satchel was bulging with envelopes of black-and-white photographs. The photographs were of Dinner, the ones that Stuart had taken. Because they were shot for reference, compositionally they weren't terribly fascinating. A simple sheet served as the backdrop for most of them. And many of the photographs were razor-sharp close-ups of Dinner's muzzle, paws, ears, tail.

The photographs wouldn't have been interesting at all to most people—unless you were the artist whose tool they were to become, or the owner of the dog.

Fanny pored over the photographs, rapt in the world contained in the glossy three-and-a-half-by-five-inch rectangles. This was her dog—every hair of her—in all her glory. It was amazing to Fanny how black-and-white photographs, when they were done well, could appear more lifelike than color photographs. Stuart's expert use of shadow and light defined Dinner beautifully and distinctly.

In a few of the photographs, Dinner's coat looked like bushy fields of wheat, her ears like tufted mountains. In others, her teeth—white lunar peaks—were dazzling against the dark cave of her open mouth. Her eyes were always radiant.

"May I have a few of these?" Fanny asked. "I mean, when you're done using them."

"I think that can be arranged," Henry replied. "And in the meanwhile, you may have this." He presented Fanny with a small, flat, wrapped package.

"I love the paper," Fanny commented. The background of the wrapping paper was a milky yellow color, and it was dotted with dogs of all sorts and kinds. Spaniels, retrievers, terriers, collies, poodles. The dogs were printed in chestnut, orange, and black, and they stood on mint green, oval patches of grass as if the dogs were all posing in tinted spotlights. It was precisely the kind of paper that Fanny used to search out to wrap presents for Henry. The choosing of this paper had been a conscious effort, she was certain.

"May I open it now?" Fanny asked, her thumb already prying the tape off.

"Of course."

Painstakingly, she opened it, so that she could save the wrapping paper. Sandwiched between two thin squares of cardboard lay another photograph of Dinner.

"I took this one myself," said Henry. "I'm not quite as good as Stuart. I was going to give it to you for your birthday, but I figured—why wait? I thought you could use it now."

Fanny trembled, she loved it so. It was exquisite: a portrait of Dinner wearing a fancy, crownlike adornment. Stars and spangles and limp stalks of white beads spun out from a band that was fastened snugly to her head. She appeared to be completely self-possessed, poised, staring off into the distance, a clairvoyant's stare.

"Thank you, Dad," she said breathlessly.

"I know you like the Snow Queen. This is my attempt at re-creating her as a dog. For you."

"Where did you get the crown?" Fanny asked.

"I noticed it hooked onto the banister when I first arrived at Stuart's. It belonged to his granddaughter, who was visiting. She didn't mind one bit when I asked if I could borrow it. And Dinner didn't mind one bit, either. She let me put it on without a hint of a struggle, and she wore it proudly as if it were hers and she had picked it out herself."

"Did Mom see it before you wrapped it?"

Henry shook his head. "No, but I'm sure she'll think it's wonderful, too."

"I can't wait to show it to her."

Turning his wrist and glancing at his watch, Henry said, "She should be home soon." Then he scowled at her playfully. "But now I have to come up with something else for your birthday next month."

He was in such a good mood that Fanny nearly kidded: How about another dog? But she stopped herself. "I don't think you can top this," she said instead. "Except for Dinner, this is the best thing I have. The best thing that's mine."

"Good," said Henry, and he gathered all the other photographs and went off to his attic room to work.

One week passed and then another, and Henry painted in his studio with great fervor, like a motor in a busy machine. He was not one to show anyone a painting in progress, but Fanny knew that he was pleased with the way his work was developing. He couldn't hide things like that; there were too many telltale signs: a cheery disposition, energetic humming wafting from the studio, and a tendency to prepare a fancy evening meal several times a week.

While Henry painted, Fanny learned how to knit. She had asked her mother to teach her.

"I'd love to," Ellen had replied, obviously surprised and tickled. "I'd given up on you and knitting. You used to say it was too old-fashioned. What changed your mind?"

Fanny knew that she was blushing. She could feel her cheeks growing pink, pinker. "I don't know," she answered. "I just decided that I'd like to learn."

On the first night of lessons, after Fanny had done her homework, she learned the basics: how to hold the needles; how to cast on stitches by positioning the fingers on her left hand like a bird's beak, twisting the yarn around her hand, plucking the yarn off with the needles and pulling it tightly, but not too tightly; how to knit; how to purl; how to cast off; and how to form a tidy ball out of a skein of yarn.

By the time she was ready for bed, Fanny had created an uneven, holey swatch the size of a pot holder that curled up at the edges.

"You're a knitter," Ellen declared, eyeing Fanny's handiwork.

"I'm not nearly as good as someone I know," Fanny said, thinking of Timothy Hill.

"Thank you," said Ellen. "But don't forget, I've been doing this for years."

For her maiden project, Fanny decided to make a scarf. A red scarf. And she chose to knit it using the seed stitch. Knit, purl, knit, purl, knit, purl, knit.

Faithful Dinner was always at Fanny's feet, often asleep under a tangle of Fanny's yarn.

Ellen had begun a complicated Norwegian sweater in multiple colors. She didn't have to watch her fingers the way Fanny did, and Ellen's needles clicked swiftly and in a pleasant rhythm. "Are you going to keep the scarf, or give it to someone?"

"I don't know," said Fanny, deep in thought. "By the time I finish, it probably won't be scarf weather anymore."

Once, as their needles rattled away, Fanny asked her mother the question that had been burning inside her, the question that she had been waiting for the perfect time to ask. "Are you ever afraid of me?" she forced herself to say, her eyes bonded to her silvery needles, her fingers rigid.

"Afraid of you? Why in the world would I be afraid of you?"

"Just a dumb question" was the only response Fanny could offer.

Ellen continued to knit. "Never," she said. "I've never been afraid of you."

"Me neither," said Fanny. "I mean—you know what I mean."

Just then, as if she were responding to a cue, Dinner yawned and moaned, and Ellen and Fanny laughed.

15

❄

Henry had completed the first painting in his new series. "You're the only one to see this so far," said Henry, wiping his glasses on his shirttail. He fussed with the wire bows, turning them on their hinges. "Come on, come in. I thought it would be appropriate for you to be the first . . ."

Fanny stepped into the studio and walked over to the easel. She didn't speak for the longest time; she was looking.

The painting was beautiful and mysterious and stately

and haunting. It was both strange and familiar. It was similar to the drawings Henry had done earlier. Dinner was huddled beneath a table. Upturned dishes—broken and not—cluttered the tabletop and floor. Dark, dense brush covered the middle ground. The leaves were oily and black like the leaves Fanny imagined in the gnarled forests of fairy tales. A stormy sky was visible behind the foliage; there was a yellowy green cast to the light. But the thing that Fanny kept coming back to was this: a glass of milk on the table, with a piece of red licorice sticking out of it.

Saying "I like it" or "It's nice" would have been all wrong, so Fanny just nodded and said all the right things without talking.

Henry understood.

"Do you have a name for it?" she inquired after minutes had passed.

"I'm glad you asked," said Henry. "I'm calling it *My Daughter's Dinner*."

Fanny nodded again, this time beaming. It dawned on her that she had something—Dinner—that he needed. She bit her lower lip. "I'm glad you told me," she said, smiling again.

It was a Saturday late in February, and Fanny had seen him out the window. It was the red cap that had caught her attention. She had spent the morning in her room making a new Marie from the thin cardboard and paper that Henry had used to wrap the Snow Queen photograph of Dinner. Fanny cut and glued and drew with felt-tip markers to create a substitute, very unlike the original doll. This one had a head that resembled Dinner's, angel wings, a doggy-print-wrapping-paper gown, and a tail with real dog hair added for authenticity. Initially, Fanny had felt silly doing it, something so childish. But she convinced herself that it was a necessary task, and so she proceeded. She even enjoyed herself. When she had finished, she folded the doll's legs so that she could sit, and she placed her on her dresser. Out in the open. Stashing her inside the file cabinet would not have been suitable.

Fanny had been on her way downstairs to check on lunch when she had seen Timothy through the window on the green.

"Do you mind if I go out?" she called to her mother.

"Do you want to eat lunch first?" Ellen asked from another room.

"No, I'm not really hungry," Fanny said, her jacket already on.

"Bye," Fanny thought she heard her mother say.

Fanny and Dinner shot out the door and glided down the sidewalk at a brisk clip. It smelled like spring outside—damp and fishy and sunny all at once. Fanny sensed the stirrings of things beneath the ground. Already, in the garden, the bright green beginnings of the tulips and crocuses were poking up through the dead leaves and badges of ice. But it was still only February, so Fanny knew that today was just a tease.

"Hi!" Fanny cried, waving. When they had crossed the street and reached the green, Fanny unhooked Dinner from her leash. Dinner bounded throughout the park, enthusiastically sniffing things seen and unseen.

Timothy pulled his cap off and wagged it high above his head.

When they were close enough to hear each other without shouting, Timothy said shyly, "I was hoping you'd see me."

"You can knock on the door, you know," said Fanny. "If you want."

Timothy shrugged and blushed and grinned. "No hockey today," he said, gesturing toward the rink. "I brought my stick and skates. They're under the bench."

The weather had been so warm lately that the ice had been melting. Water puddled on what remained of the hard surface, reflecting the sun.

Some neighborhood kids were breaking off chunks of ice from the mounds surrounding the rink and tossing them into the puddles.

"A bomb! A bomb!" one screamed.

"It's the end of the world!" yelled another.

A third shrieked, "Whooo-whooo! This is not a test!"

Fanny and Timothy walked over to the bench. They sat and watched the children, laughing and not saying much. Dinner ran up to the bench periodically to check on Fanny. Then, after a play bow, she'd dart off excitedly, dodging between shrubs, hunting squirrels, splashing in the water—in general, acting like a puppy.

"She's great," said Timothy.

"Yeah," said Fanny.

The silences didn't seem awkward to Fanny. She closed her eyes and raised her head to the sun. She was thinking of so many things at the same time, her mind had to work hard to keep them all straight. She was thinking about her father's painting and her half-finished scarf and the new Marie. She was thinking of Mary Dibble and Timothy, Timothy, Timothy Hill. She wondered when she would get the photograph of Dinner as the Snow Queen back from the frame shop. She wondered what it would be like to have met her own parents when they were her age. If by some trick of time they all could have been twelve together, would they have been friends, the three of them? Imagine that!

Will the rink refreeze? And will I be able to skate a figure eight this year?

Should we walk over to Mary's house?

Should I show Timothy the scarf?

"Hey," said Timothy, nudging her gently with his elbow. "Wake up. I want you to see something." He pulled a square lump of paper out of his pocket and unfolded it. It was a page from a garden catalog. "Look, you can order ladybugs," he said, leaning into her. "Two thousand for fifteen dollars. I'm going to do it. Ladybugs are good bugs, you know. They devour aphids. They help a garden."

Fanny giggled. She hadn't known one could order bugs through the mail, much less ever met someone who wanted to do it.

"You think it's weird," Timothy remarked quietly, wadding the paper and stuffing it back into his pocket.

"No, not at all. It's kind of neat."

"I might want to do something with science. Or bugs," Timothy said, scratching his nose, then hiding behind his hand. "If I can't play professional hockey."

"I'd like to be a linguist," Fanny told him. She had never mentioned this to anyone. Hearing her own words startled her a bit.

"That would be a great career," he said solemnly. "Cool."

He seems genuinely impressed, she thought. Someone like Bruce Rankin would have said, "*Linguine?* Fanny Swann wants to be *linguine* when she grows up!"

She wished to do more than learn languages and study the origins of words. Although she didn't know if it was part of the job, she hoped to create new words, too. And she already had one word to her credit.

The smallest of the neighborhood doomsayers came toddling over, with Dinner close behind. His name was Corey Shinkle. His clothes were filthy and wet, but his face was flushed and buoyant. Placing one dimpled pink hand on Fanny's thigh and the other on Timothy's knee, he shouted gleefully, "It really *is* the end of the world!"

She smiled kindly at him, her teeth showing. She knew that it wasn't the end of the world. In fact, the end of the world was the furthest thing from her mind. She was happy for now. And now was all that mattered.

Corey Shinkle ran off, his arms outstretched, belching forth a wretched sound like a fighter plane. Dinner followed him, then circled back to Fanny and Timothy. She sat squarely in front of Fanny, waiting.

"What do you want to do?" Timothy asked.

"Hmmm," Fanny breathed. She bent down so that she was nose to nose with Dinner. She looked intently into Dinner's clear, brown eyes. The options were limitless.